THE HELL'S HALF ACRE TRADE

PART 2 OF THE ST. ISIDORE SERIES

DARIA MIGOUNOVA

Part 2 of the St. Isidore Series

"Attention to detail; commitment to quality." -- Niagara Co.

Copyright © 2021 Daria Migounova
All rights reserved.

All rights reserved. No part of this publication may be reproduced, stored in a retrieval system, or transmitted, in any form or by any means, without the prior written consent of the publisher.

ACKNOWLEDGMENTS

My gratitude to my husband Boris, the first reader (technically listener) of this novel and relentless fan. Thank you for your endless support and for your sports knowledge. Special thanks to my one of my oldest friends, Deborah-Lynn, with whom I've concocted this tale many years ago. This story would not exist without your contributions and I sincerely hope you enjoy the final version. Finally, a huge thank you to my family for encouraging me and being the fearless early readers of this novel.

CONTENTS

1. Initiation — 1
2. St. Isidore: Part VI. Casa Nové — 6
3. Execution — 13
4. Danger — 40
5. [REDACTED] — 48
6. Interrogatorio — 57
7. Motivation — 87
8. Return — 92
9. St. Isidore – Part VII. Abandonment — 102
10. St. Isidore – Part VIII. Up in Smoke — 114
11. Betrayal — 127
12. The Trade — 164
13. Deadhorse — 186
14. Dissolution — 196
15. September — 212

Part Three of the St. Isidore Series — 231
About the Author — 233

ONE
INITIATION

- Niagara Falls, NY. February 19, 2014 -

A forceful winter storm raged outside the windows of the Polar Parlor's second floor office, flurries of scattered snowflakes hurrying in every direction on gales of river wind. Sebastian was leaning up against the mahogany desk, unreadable expression on his face.

Noa sat in one of the office chairs, computer in his lap. He watched as the other members of the Niagara Co. entered the room.

"Hey, sugar," Elli came in first, taking a seat on the windowpane. Nick, who sat in a chair on the other side of the room, soon followed.

Mike rushed inside, dusting snow off his hat, "What's going on, Boss? Are we under attack?" He took a seat across from the desk, beside Noa.

"I reckon we'd know if we were under attack," Elli said. Then, hesitantly, "we're not, are we? I don't like that look, Bassie."

Sebastian exhaled. "I suppose you could call it an attack of sorts."

The woman from the Bella Luna alleyway trailed in last, after Mike. Noa now knew her name to be Lucy. She said nothing, taking her post by the window next to Elli. She wore a long trench coat and a surprisingly bright pink scarf, tied snugly around her neck.

Nick sat up, all ears. "Manhattan?"

Sebastian gave a slight nod. "Noa, if you would."

Tense from nerves and the five pairs of eyes awaiting his next move, Noa hurriedly opened his laptop and placed it on the desk for the others to see the screen. The grainy footage of an empty storeroom filled the display.

Elli gasped, "We've been robbed? Either that, or you're finally doing spring cleaning as I keep suggesting."

Mike leaned in, looking at the monitor. "But this place didn't store anything special, did it? Who would rob it?"

"It was Rossini, wasn't it?" Nick said with a snarl. "That piece of shit."

Rossini? Noa searched the archives of his recent memory. He recalled seeing the name from his tangential investigation into the Venetian mafia while he was researching Sebastian's mysterious origins. He had crossed the ocean to New York City and controlled a large portion of the mob, at one time.

Is it the same one? Involved with Niagara Co.? Noa flinched when Sebastian's gloved hand came to rest on his shoulder.

"It was Rossini. Thanks to Noa, we can make the first move," he said.

"Way to go, hon'!" Elli smiled. "So, what now?"

Noa winced as the grip on his shoulder tightened.

"Well," Sebastian said in a low voice. "It has become clear that something must be done about him, since he is sending me this message."

Nick pounded a closed fist into his open palm. "Yes! About time. We have all that new ammo sittin' around, collecting dust – can I finally use it?"

Elli rolled her eyes, wrapping an arm around Lucy with a dramatic gesture. "Right, but there's a reason it's collecting dust. Besides, why would we send you, Nicky, when we've got this lovely lady?"

Lucy absentmindedly stroked the knitted hem of her scarf. "I can terminate him," she said in a voice that hovered just above a whisper.

Noa made an effort to keep his reactions to a minimum. He heaved a mental sigh of relief when Sebastian released his shoulder and went behind the desk.

"Let's park that for now," he said, taking a seat. "Elli, who's watching the Parlor at the moment?" Sebastian locked eyes with her for a second.

"Mike said it was an emergency— ah." Elli hummed in confirmation. She let go of Lucy, turning her attention to the redhead. "Noa, sugar, can you cover the counter for a bit?"

"Now? But I—" he protested only to be cut off by Elli's finger suddenly pressed against his mouth. She kneeled down beside him.

"Now. Thanks, hon'." She poked him on the nose gently.

Noa looked around the room. Defeated, he packed up his laptop and left with a sulk. As he shut the door behind him, Mike called out:

"Don't eavesdrop this time, kiddo."

Behind the frosted purple and white counter of the Polar Parlor, Noa stared at the falling snow beyond the glass and fumed.

How he would have loved to be a fly on the wall of the conversation taking place upstairs! Granted, it didn't seem to have anything to do with insider trading, but still it was an opportunity to see how they operated. How they plot revenge – how often can one witness *that*?

Oh, no. Noa blinked, halting his own train of thought. He wasn't excited by this, was he?

No, of course not, he reasoned, *I'm just investigating.* Clearly, they're planning something illegal. He glanced at the staff-access door. Something undoubtedly illegal, devious, and *cool— no!*

Stop thinking like that! Noa shook his head subconsciously, leaving the counter and starting to pace the length of the Parlor's floor.

What are they planning? He gazed up at the ceiling, decorated with its twine-hung silver snowflakes, while pacing back and forth.

Nick mentioned new ammunition. The quiet woman, Lucy, said she would kill outright. A gang of criminals, nothing less. Noa repeated the fact to himself, finding that it would occasionally slip his mind.

How could it not? Most of his time with the Niagara Co., to date, has been spent helping Elli, or joining her for a card game with Mike. Even the few interactions he's had with Sebastian have been friendly.

They treated each other as friends. Or rather, as family. Noa felt the unspoken trust between each of the members in the room upstairs; he yearned for a similar connection.

He stopped pacing. Not with *them,* surely.

Noa sat at a pink table and groaned, semi-hoping a customer would enter the shop to distract him. As a last resort, he spent his idle time fixing the PecanBot.

After an agonizingly long forty-five minutes, Mike called Noa back up to the office.

TWO
ST. ISIDORE: PART VI. CASA NOVÉ

- New York City. Winter, 2007 -

The putrid smell of gasoline and smoke lingered in the air. Iron and salt. The lights, flickering, cast billowing shadows on the stained, splintering surroundings.

"I'm bigger now. I'm stronger now."

Bullet shells and bodies litter the floor. Screams and curses echo down the halls.

"This is *my* domain."

A man is pushed against a wall, fear reflecting in his eyes. A hand grabs him by the throat. He strains against it.

"Nové. How can you do this to me? After I took you in!"

A scoff.

"Please take a bow, Gio. I am your work of art." The sound of a flicked lighter.

The man shuddered at the sight before him. A beautiful, raven-haired devil with blue lightning in his eyes.

"Are you going to kill me?"

"Shouldn't I?"

"I gave you everything." It was a desperate tone. "I spoiled you rotten!"

A bitter laugh.

"Definitely rotten. You shouldn't have come here, Gio. All that glitters is not gold – didn't you know?"

"Please, just spare my life! Have mercy on me. I'll work for you."

A plea.

A consideration.

"Beg some more. I'll think about it."

- New York City. Thursday, February 20, 2014 -

9:30pm

The next day, huddled around an overly extravagant hotel room coffee table, Mike brought his hands together in a loud clap.

"Alright, kiddo. So, you understand the plan?"

"I think so."

"Great!" Mike patted the map on the table. "Do you want to go over it one more time?"

Noa paused. "I think so."

"No problem," Mike chuckled. "It's a-okay to be nervous on your first assignment, buddy. I'm sure you'll do just fine." He rearranged some papers in front of them, pointing to a diagram on a floorplan. "This is where the Boss and Ross – ha! That rhymes! – are gonna meet."

Noa followed along as Mike indicated a yellow circle labeled 'S' situated in a room across from a red square marked with an 'R' on the fourth floor of an office building.

"I've been meaning to ask," Noa said earnestly. "Who is this Rossini guy? Do you have history with him?"

"No, not us, exactly," Mike scratched the back of his head. "The Boss does though. From what he told me, the two of them used to work together. Wait, no, that's not right. Seb worked *for* the guy, back in the day."

"Really?" Noa found it hard to imagine Sebastian taking orders from anyone. "What happened?"

Mike lowered his voice to a whisper, despite the absence of anyone else in the room other than Noa. "The Boss took over. In a pretty brutal coup, from what I heard. But I only know stories, since I met him after all that happened."

Noa scanned his mind for the images of Giovanni Rossini he found during his research. "Isn't Rossini much older? How did their positions flip like that?"

"I don't know, but it must've been epic!" Mike said with a grin. "Now, can we continue?"

Noa nodded.

"Cool. So, you and El' will be across the street: here," he pointed to two triangles labeled 'E' and 'N' on the upper floor of a warehouse. "Your job is to get into the mainframe or whatchamacallit of the office building and kill the lights in the meetin' room."

Mike pointed to two more circles on either side of the diagram, near Sebastian and Rossini. "When you do that, Nick and Lucy will take over. But the lights have to stay out, got it?"

Noa raised his hand. "What if Rossini brings back-up?"

"Oh, he'll definitely have men with him," Mike said. "But that's fine. They won't know what hit 'em in the dark. Seb will give the signal to Elli, and once you hit the lights, *boom,* Nick and Luce'll finish the job."

"Uh huh." Noa nodded along. "By the way, is Lucy some kind of assassin?"

"Don't call her that!" Mike blurted out. "She's amazing, really," he said with a wistful sigh. "And super sweet once you get to know her. You shouldn't treat her different or be scared of her just 'cause of her army background – she would never hurt one of her own."

Noa tried to prod further. "She was in the army?"

"She doesn't really like to talk about it," Mike said, unsmiling. "Now, you ready?"

The agent swallowed nervously. "Ready."

"Good." Mike packed up the papers, handing them to Noa. "I'll take you to the machine thingamabobs where you can work your magic, but I won't be staying. I'll be with the Boss across the street. Elli will stay with you the whole time, though, and give you the signal."

Noa nodded once more, grabbing his computer and the diagrams.

Mike stood, heading for the exit. "It's showtime!"

Down the corridor from Mike's room, in the penthouse suite of the Downtown New York Four Seasons hotel, Sebastian stood by the closet safe, reading a newspaper. The Newspaper.

He carefully skimmed the breaking news story of the front page once more, eyes scanning the text for a final time, before putting it back in its place.

With a somber sigh, he locked the safe.

A knock sounded at the door. "Chief? We're ready to go," Nick shouted from the hall.

"Coming."

On the topmost floor of an unoccupied warehouse, Noa hovered over a wall-mounted switchboard, carefully attaching cables to his laptop.

In less than fifteen minutes, Sebastian would be meeting Rossini in a building across the street. His heart was racing. Why was he even here?

He glanced back at Elli. She was sitting cross-legged on the floor in front of the window, configuring a headset. She adjusted its connection and spoke into the mic a few times.

"Ten-four," she said, standing suddenly and repositioning herself against the wall on the other side of the room.

Noa flipped a final switch and wiped his forehead with the back of his sleeve. "Okay, I think I'm done." He turned his laptop to Elli, which displayed a video feed of the room in which Sebastian and Rossini were to meet.

"Good job, hon'," Elli smiled. "Make sure you stay focused and don't move from that spot, okay? The lights have to go off or else baldy will get the upper hand."

"Yes, ma'am!" Noa sat on his knees by the switchboard, watching the video display on the computer screen.

He felt an odd sense of power knowing that his actions would determine the outcome of this encounter. No one aside from Elli, who was on the other side of the warehouse room, could stop him. Noa could simply *pretend* to press the wrong button.

He could easily sabotage the whole mission.

But, when Sebastian and a large, bald man entered the onscreen display, Noa anxiously anticipated the moment that he would press the right button after all.

I don't care about their approval, he thought, *or safety. They'll kill me if I don't.*

"Hon', when I give the signal, hit the lights," Elli said. "Ready?"

He nodded, watching the screen. The video feed had no sound, but he could see that Sebastian and Rossini were having a heated conversation. As expected, Rossini had two men at his sides. Mike stood beside Sebastian, but after some time he abruptly left the room.

"Okay." Elli inhaled a nervous breath. "Get set..."

Noa readied his left hand over the trackpad, biting his lip.

"Now!" Elli shouted.

He flipped the switch. The meeting room went dark.

Then, in a second, the lights turned back on.

"Shit," Noa gasped, "A back-up generat—"

BOOM!!

The display on the computer screen was lost immediately just as the windows in the warehouse room shattered with a spectacular force.

Propelled by the blast, Noa and Elli flew backwards several feet. Noa hit the back wall; Elli fell into a pile of empty boxes.

Regaining her balance, she got up quickly and ran over to Noa. "Are you okay, hon'?" She crouched down beside him.

He winced, opening his eyes. "I-I pressed the switch,

Elli! There was a back-up generator, I didn't know! What happened?"

Elli hugged Noa to her chest, rubbing his back. "Shh, it's okay. I knew you would do it. I just knew it." He couldn't see it, but Elli was smiling.

Noa pulled away, getting up unsteadily. "What happened, Elli? What was that explosion?" Turning to face the window, he instantly collapsed back to the ground.

"No..."

The building across the street, the one in which Sebastian and Rossini and Nick and Mike and Lucy must have been a moment ago, now had a hole in its side the size of a wrecking ball. Fire engulfed the walls, licking up the crumbling façade. Raging flames and debris obscured the interior.

"Oh, god." Noa trembled, unable to hold back burning tears. His heart hammered in his chest. "Is this my fault? Elli! Are they dead?"

He was embraced again as Elli's hand shielded his eyes. "It's okay, sugar. It's okay. You did good."

THREE
EXECUTION

- Niagara Falls, The Day Before -

Nobody spoke for a few minutes in the Polar Parlor's second floor office. The clock on the back wall ticked noisily as the winter wind howled beyond the windows.

Elli returned to her seat, leaning against Lucy's shoulder and scrolling through her phone.

Nick cleared his throat. "Are we good?"

Finally, Mike opened the door just a crack and peeked into the hallway.

"All clear," he said with a thumbs-up.

"Good." Sebastian sat up, leaning his elbows on the oak desk. "So. We now know that Gio Rossini has decided to rob me. Us, I mean." He paused. "Mostly me."

"Why now, all of a sudden?" Elli asked, glancing at him over her phone. "And why that place? I don't remember anything important being stored there, either."

Sebastian gave a slight shrug. "It's symbolic."

"Beg pardon?" she raised her eyebrows. "Was it an imaginary heist?"

"If I'm not mistaken, today marks the seven-year anniversary of my takeover," he replied. "The final battle went down in that room. It used to be a restaurant cover for the Mala del Brenta. Now it's just a storage facility."

"Would Ross really steal from you because of somethin' so abstract, Boss?" Mike asked, taking a seat in Noa's chair.

"No, it makes sense," Nick said. "Symbolism and shit – that's a big thing for traditional-type mobsters. Rossini probably thinks it's some grand gesture."

"Then can't we just ignore it?" Mike asked hopefully. "I mean, nothing important was stolen, right?"

An awkward silence lingered in the room.

"No? Anyone?"

"It's a matter of principle, Mike," Sebastian said calmly. "I can't let it slide."

"Well, you *can*," Elli twirled her hair. "But you won't."

"He will just come back for more," he said. "Regardless of how you want to phrase it, I have a plan that can kill two birds with one stone. A way to confront Rossini and initiate our newest recruit."

"Don't make him do anything diabolical, Bassie," Elli said nervously. "Don't make that poor boy into a murderer."

"Or a thief!" Mike added. "He's just a kid."

"Pah!" Nick scoffed. "Let the man speak, would you?"

"Don't worry. It'll be as easy as flipping a switch," Sebastian said with a smile. "Here's the plan."

The plan was relatively simple.

Sebastian Nové and Gio Rossini were going to arrange an in-person meeting in New York. It would be somewhere nice but discreet, in an unused office tower in the East Village.

The meeting would be set with no pretenses, although

all parties clearly knew the reason. They would agree to meet the following day, after nightfall.

Rossini would likely bring backup. Sebastian would have backup as well. From another location, Noa would be instructed to remotely turn off the meeting room lights upon receiving a signal. Once the room was dark, Nick and Lucy, who would be hidden in the hallway, would quickly dispose of Rossini and his men.

The test to determine Noa's loyalty to the group rested upon his decision to flip the switch. If the lights stayed on after Sebastian's signal, then he would have his answer. If the lights went out, then Noa passed the test.

Everyone in the room agreed to the idea and began preparations.

Sebastian didn't know at the time, however, that the plan would undergo some slight adjustments soon.

- New York City. Thursday, February 20, 2014 –

11:00pm

Noa was still trembling as he made his way through the shattered glass and debris with Elli by his side. They slowly crept out of the warehouse and onto the street, towards the burning building.

Elli held a protective arm around him, using her other hand to press the earpiece of her headset closer, hoping to hear something other than static.

"I don't understand," Noa kept repeating in a whisper. "What happened?"

They stopped before the exploded remains of a foundation that stood just minutes ago. The entrance doors had collapsed, and the fire was spreading.

"It's okay, hon'. I'm sure they're fine." Elli peered into the building, coughing from the smoke.

"How do you know?" Noa's voice shook as he stared at the flames. "What if they're dead?" He made an attempt to approach the unstable brick but seized up with fear, taking a step back.

Elli put her hands on his shoulders, offering a comforting smile. "Noa, sugar. Do you think we're idiots?"

He was stunned by the question. "Huh?"

"I asked a question. Do you?"

Noa blinked, eyes burning from the fumes. "I— No, I don't."

"Then you just need to have faith that we know what we're doing." She wiped some tears from his cheek. "I bet you a thousand ice cream sundaes that Nick will come running out right now, yelling profanities."

As if by script, Noa heard shouting from the building's alleyway. His head whipped around to see Nick and Lucy running towards them.

"God *fucking* damn it!" Nick seethed, returning his gun to its holster. "I was one burrito short of ruining these pants. I hate explosions."

"See?" Elli patted Noa's shoulders. "What did I tell you?"

He stared at them, dumbfounded. Nick's usual white attire was pristine, and Lucy's bright pink scarf was unscathed. There was no evidence that they had been in a fire of any kind.

"I don't understand," Noa finally managed to say. "I thought you two were inside."

Nick shrugged. "In the eleventh hour, as it were, the

Boss told us to leave the building. We went to the adjacent ones, sniping through the windows."

"I got a last-minute change too," Elli said. "Bassie told me to move away from the windows, and to ensure Noa stayed away from them as well."

Nick furrowed his brows. "Wait. So, he knew Rossini was packin' bombs?"

Distraught, Noa turned to the fiery rubble once more. "If he told you two to get out, that means he and Mike stayed inside when it exploded?!"

Lucy stiffened, following Noa's line of sight. She soon breathed a sigh of relief, however, when Mike came stumbling out of the alley.

"Thank god, you guys are here!" He exclaimed, sprinting over. "What the hell happened? Seb told me to get him some briefcase from the car and as soon as I was outside, BOOM goes the dynamite! Literally!"

"He told you too leave, too?" Elli's voice trailed off.

The five of them exchanged worried glances. Sirens blared in the distance.

"He knew it would explode?" Noa took a hesitant step towards the burning building, then another. "Sebastian is still in there!"

"Chill kid, you can relax now," Nick said. "You got the lights, I saw 'em go off for a sec. You passed, to my surprise."

"Passed?" Noa shook his head, "What are you talking about? We have to go look for him!" Shaking, he tried once more to approach the flames, but was picked up swiftly by the back of his jacket. Lucy held him a couple feet above the ground, moving him away from the blaze.

Noa flailed, "Put me down!"

"Shh!" Elli grasped her headset, listening intently. A

relieved expression washed over her face. "Let's get back to the hotel, guys. The fire department will be here soon."

- New York City, Earlier That Day -

8:00pm

With the location for Rossini's meeting finalized and Noa's initiation setup complete, Sebastian stood by the window of his hotel room with a glass of wine, considering possible scenarios of the night to come.

He knew that Rossini would not come alone, or empty handed, but Sebastian figured it was time to end their silly feud. He had let Rossini do as he pleased in Manhattan over the years, almost as a pity, considering his mob was consolidated into the Niagara Company years ago. But the time for pity was over if Rossini had the audacity to make a statement.

Sebastian positioned his team on a mental chess board. Nick and Lucy would be hidden from sight in the hall, ready to shoot. Mike would be at his side, as always. Elli would be in direct communication, ready for his signal, in the building across the street. Noa would be with her, manning the switchboard.

Rossini wouldn't have time to pull a gun, and snipers were unlikely. And while a bomb did cross Sebastian's mind, he had mistakenly assumed that Gio Rossini was not suicidal.

As for Noa, the test was elegantly simple. Either he turns the lights off or not. If he decides not to, he could say they malfunctioned, or he pressed the wrong button, or he missed. The only person with him would be Elli, so he would not feel threatened at any point. He could run if he so chose.

Sebastian had a fairly high confidence in Noa's passing. He hoped the boy would pass.

With some time to kill before the meeting, Sebastian decided to arrange some financial calls to clients. He opened the safe and retrieved the Newspaper, placing it on the hotel desk. The paper was flipped to the business news column, as it always was.

But, as he laid it down, he caught a glimpse of the front-page headline.

New York City building collapses after explosion - millions in property damage

By SUSAN GREENE

An abandoned building collapsed in a fiery burst of rubble on Thursday and flames spread to nearby buildings in what officials said appeared to be a criminal-related explosion, scattering debris across surrounding streets in the heart of Manhattan's fashionable East Village.

Orange flames billowed and smoke could be seen and smelled for miles after the blaze, in an area of old tenement buildings that are home to students and longtime residents in an area near New York University and Washington Square Park.

About 250 firefighters converged to fight the flames, and the fire department's commissioner said a second building was "in danger of possible collapse" and four buildings were affected in all.

Mayor Bill de Blasio said the blast appeared to have been purposeful and is suspicious of foul play.

noted that no one had reported a gas leak to authorities before Thursday's blast.

Gladys Yello, who lives a block away, ran outside when she heard "a huge boom."

"Already there was smoke everywhere" when she saw the building, she said. "The flames were coming out from the roof. The fire was coming out of every window."

Items from a ground-floor sushi restaurant were blown into a street, and the explosion was so forceful that it blew the door off a cafe across the avenue. Rubble, glass and debris littered sidewalks.

Con Ed crews planned to start investigating after firefighters got the blaze under control. The state Department of Public Service was monitoring Con Ed's response, Gov. Andrew Cuomo said.

In the aftermath, an anonymous witness stated that they saw 5 "suspicious-looking" individuals fleeing the scene. They said the people appeared "pretty young, one might've been a kid."

"We can confirm that there has been an explosion at this address and we are currently investigating all the aspects ... with respect to how an explosion could have transpired at this address," said Peter Hamilton, an investigator with the Office of the New York Fire Marshal, on Thursday.

His breath caught in his throat. He re-read the article three times – there was no mistaking it. This was definitely the building in which him and Rossini were meeting in a few hours.

He folded the paper under his arm, pacing the room. His confidence in Noa's success decreased drastically but he was calmed by the mention of 'five suspicious-looking individuals' fleeing the scene.

The Newspaper proved that any adjustments to the plan would keep his team safe.

He focused on the newfound knowledge. If Rossini was bringing explosives, when would he set them off? At the very least, Sebastian would have to rearrange Lucy and Nick to a different location and move Elli and Noa away from any glass. He would also need to predict the right moment to send Mike outside, to avoid raising suspicion.

Then, alone with Rossini, Sebastian would give the signal to Elli. She would pass it to Noa. Assuming Rossini catches on, and assuming Noa fails, this would be the moment of the explosion.

Sebastian stopped pacing. He couldn't help but frown, having truly hoped Noa would succeed.

There was just one piece of the puzzle remaining: Sebastian himself. He would be in the room with Rossini, who may or may not set off a suicidal blast. He could not imagine an explosion that large would not annihilate its detonator in the process.

Unfortunately, this did not bode well for anyone in close vicinity.

Sebastian fell back on the hotel bed, holding the Newspaper over his chest. This wouldn't do. Dying meant losing – to Rossini of all people – and he did not like to lose.

- New York City. Thursday, February 20, 2014 -

11:30pm

"Was that him?" Noa gasped. "He's alive?!"

Elli removed her headset with a wide grin. "Yes! And he wanted to see you, so let's hurry back."

As the sound of sirens grew louder, the five of them squeezed into Nick's getaway car and raced downtown. Nick barely had a chance to switch the gear to 'park' before Noa jumped out of the backseat and sped into the Four Seasons.

He made a beeline for the elevators, apologizing to any nighttime guests that he bumped into along the way, and impatiently stabbed at the penthouse floor button.

"Come on, come on, come on," he grumbled.

"Ahem." A woman in a fur coat cleared her throat, eyeing the boy condescendingly. "You can't access that floor without a keycard, young man."

Noa groaned, rifling in his pockets. To the woman's astonishment, he whipped out a black plastic card and slammed it against the sensor.

"My," she said. "Perhaps I shall stay at Trump Tower next time."

When the elevator announced its arrival at the top floor, Noa rushed out towards the western-most room. He sprinted down the hall, the sudden movement sending pangs of pain through his aching body, but his thoughts were in disarray – devoid of the investigation, of finding evidence, and of the fact that he had a scheduled CSIS communication early the next morning.

He stopped before the door. It was open, just an inch,

with the golden swing bar latch caught in the crevice preventing the door from locking.

Noa caught his breath, lungs sore. He held out his fist to knock but changed his mind instantly and pushed it open, running inside.

Sebastian stood by the window, overlooking the Hudson, with his back to the door. He was hunched over slightly and had a hand braced against the wall.

"Noa, before you say anything, I—" he started but was immediately interrupted by Noa's brisk approach.

"You're alive!" he cried in disbelief. "I thought you exploded and died!"

Sebastian gave a brief chuckle before wincing. "Takes more than that to kill me."

In the window's reflection, Noa could see he was holding some kind of towel against his chest. Noa took a step back, giving him room to turn around.

Sebastian was not in his usual attire. Instead of the sleek black suit, he wore plain jeans and a white shirt, which hung loosely, unbuttoned. He peeled back the towel compress with a grimace, glancing down to evaluate the damage.

Noa reflexively covered his mouth with his hand. "Oh my god," he breathed. "This is all my fault!"

Starting at the upper-left side of Sebastian's collarbone, a large reddish burn obscured the vast majority of his chest, traveling down to his stomach in fragmented bursts of scarlet. His entire body, where visible, was covered in darkening bruises.

"Not pretty, I know," he said. "But it isn't your fault." In an attempt to comfort him, he patted Noa's head softly. "You did everything right."

"But the lights—"

"Turned off," Sebastian confirmed. "End of story. You passed, just as I thought you would."

Noa felt oddly warmed by the praise. "This was all just another test?"

"An initiation, of sorts," Sebastian said. "Now you're officially part of the team."

Noa's mind swirled with this new information. Were they expecting him to fail? Did this mean they would no longer doubt his loyalty?

"More importantly, are you alright?" Sebastian moved his hand to Noa's chin, lifting it up to inspect his face. "I didn't expect the blast to reach as far as it did. How is Elli?"

Noa pushed his hand away with a scoff. "I think you got the worst of it!"

"You should see the other guy," Sebastian said with a childishly smug expression.

"Right," Noa looked at him dubiously. "I don't suppose you're going to the ER?"

Sebastian sat on the edge of the bed with some difficulty. "Too many questions would be raised. I have a doctor colleague flying into New York from the west tomorrow, I'll be fine until then."

"You don't look fine," Noa frowned, looking around. "I'm sure there's first-aid around here somewhere. Don't you bring an emergency kit on missions or something?"

Sebastian watched curiously as the boy searched his hotel room. The burns were definitely causing him a great deal of discomfort, but he hadn't yet given much thought about treatment.

Finally, he said, "in the closet. Above the safe."

Noa retrieved the kit from the top of the locked safe, unzipping it. "What the hell? It's half empty!"

"Is it?" Sebastian asked. "Mike gets into a lot of accidents. I'll get him to re-stock it."

With a frustrated sigh, Noa returned to the bedside and rummaged through the little white box. He took out some ointment and gauze, setting them to the side.

"Noa, you don't need to do this," Sebastian protested. "Really."

Noa pointed to the exposed rosary around his neck. "Take this off," he said sternly.

Sebastian studied the boy's face with amusement. "Oh? Are you giving me orders now?"

Noa didn't waver. "If you don't then I will, which will probably hurt more."

"Alright, fair enough." Sebastian removed the rosary, tinged from the flames, and put it into his pocket. The necklace left a flushed, cross-shaped imprint in his skin.

Noa shook his head disapprovingly, starting to apply the gel. "You know, rosaries aren't meant to be worn like jewelry."

"Is that so?" Sebastian said casually, actively trying not to react to the sting of the treatment.

"You aren't really Catholic, are you?" Noa asked.

"Good deduction," he replied. "It's a keepsake of someone dear to me that passed on."

"Oh, I'm sorry," Noa said awkwardly. He kept his head down, focusing on the task at hand.

"Are your first-aid skills 'self-taught' as well?" Sebastian asked.

Avoiding eye contact, Noa realized it may have been better to feign ignorance regarding injury treatment, rather than following government agency first-aid training.

"I learned it in school," he lied, opting to change the subject. "How did you survive that explosion?"

"How do you think I did?"

Noa knitted his brows. "Well, you must have known there would be an explosion. You told Elli and I to move away from the windows, and you made the others leave the building."

"Very perceptive," Sebastian said. "What else?"

Noa found it difficult to concentrate knowing he was being watched so closely. "I'm assuming you didn't know about the backup generator, since your plan hinged on the lights turning off at the right time," he said nervously.

"Not quite. We never intended for the lights to *stay* off, so I didn't care much about the backup generator. That split second was all we needed."

Sebastian couldn't help but smile at the baffled expression that took over Noa's face.

"You mean— The lights coming back on wasn't a problem?! So, Mike and Elli lied to me?"

"No, no, we really didn't know about the generator. But it was irrelevant at that point since Rossini had already perished," Sebastian said nonchalantly. "Why, were you worried?"

Noa nearly hit him. "I thought I screwed something up!"

Their eyes met. "You did everything right," Sebastian said, "just as I hoped."

Noa stammered, "I still don't understand how you got out of there! How did you know there would be an explosion?" It took a conscious effort to keep his hands steady as he applied the cloth compress.

"I'll tell you some other time."

- New York City, Earlier That Day -

8:30pm

Sebastian only had a few hours left before the meeting. He knew that much of his actions would need to be improvised but concentrated on preparing for anything within his control.

He called Mike, and the two of them drove to the meeting site early.

"Why're we here so soon, Boss?" Mike asked, watching quizzically as Sebastian searched every corner of the rendezvous room.

"A precaution," he replied, peeking underneath the desk and inside the drawers for any explosives. "Checking if anything could have been placed here in advance."

Mike nodded in understanding, scouring the office floor. "Doesn't look like it."

Upon finding nothing, Sebastian reasoned Rossini must be bringing the bomb himself. He evaluated the space. The room was reasonably-sized, probably an executive office, with metal storage cabinets and a large wooden desk. A rectangular window overlooked the alley.

Sebastian removed his coat, tossing it aside. "Help me out, Mike," he said, pressing his hands against the cabinet and pushing it towards the door.

"What are we doing?" Mike asked but complied, pulling the other side.

"It's too cramped in there," Sebastian said. "I want to get all the furniture out."

"The desk and chairs too? Where will you guys sit?"

They pushed the cabinets into a neighboring office.

"The chairs are fine. The desk needs to go, though. I think there may be something better in storage underground."

After emptying the room of all its furniture except for the chairs, Mike followed Sebastian down to the basement. He stood by, puzzled, as Sebastian checked various unused workspaces for something. After a short search, he called Mike over.

"Can we get this to the fourth floor?" he asked, resting his palm on a sturdy, steel blacktop desk.

"Uh," Mike shrugged. "Sure! I'll get the back if you get the front."

Together, they maneuvered the table upstairs and placed it into the meeting room.

Sebastian went behind the desk and, to Mike's utter bewilderment, flipped it forward onto its front side. Then he stood it back up and flipped it again – testing the speed.

"Alright. Final touch," he said, opening the rectangular window as far as it would allow. A few puffs of resting snow blew inside, settling on the floor. "Mike, can I borrow your coat? You can use mine if you'd like."

Mike hastily lifted Sebastian's expensive jacket off the ground. "Are you sure, Boss? Mine is... Well, it's not really your style."

"Please."

"If you say so!" Mike removed his puffy winter coat, dusted it off and handed it to his boss.

"Thanks. We can head back to the hotel now for the final briefing. I'll meet you here at 10:00."

On their way to the site, while Mike went with Elli and Noa to the warehouse, Sebastian drove with Nick and Lucy to the meeting location.

"By the way," he said as they approached. "Slight change in plans. I think you two may have a better angle from these adjacent buildings." He pointed them out through the car windows. "There is a higher risk of being caught if you're too close."

The two of them agreed, setting up quickly in neighboring buildings, ensuring they had a view through the window.

Sebastian arrived back at the meeting room. It was devoid of furniture, save for the robust steel desk and two chairs on either side. The draft from the open window chilled the enclosed space. A slight shiver ran down his spine with an unwelcome momentary consideration of death.

He put on Mike's exceptionally puffy jacket just as Mike entered the room with a wave, coming to stand by Sebastian's side. He dropped his usually goofy attitude and replaced it with a serious and authoritative air.

Sebastian sat down in the chair behind the desk, listening attentively as three pairs of footsteps drew near. The article was lacking in detail, which meant that as soon as this meeting began, he would have a limited amount of time to deduce the source and detonation medium of the explosion.

Giovanni Rossini entered the room, followed by two men Sebastian recognized from his time with the Venetian mob. At first glance, he did not spot any explosive devices. The two men wore black suits and had their hands at their sides. They were likely armed, but any sudden moves would alert Nick and Lucy to shoot them first.

Rossini himself wore an oversized black jacket, keeping his hands in his pockets. His appearance hadn't changed much in nearly ten years, except for the few wrinkles that now patterned his forehead. He sat down in the chair on the other side of the table, across from Sebastian.

"Nové, as I live and breathe. The Millennial Tycoon, eh?" he said with an ingenuine laugh. "Long time, no see."

"Indeed. How long has it been?" Sebastian asked, knowing the answer perfectly well.

"Seven years. Nice number, that seven." Rossini pulled out a cigar from his right pocket. One of his men lit it instantly. "So, to what do I owe the pleasure of this meeting?"

"No need to be coy," Sebastian said. "We both know why. Although, I am disappointed. I never thought you would stoop as low as petty theft."

Rossini laughed again. "You're familiar with stooping low, aren't you? Or have you forgotten where you come from?"

"I prefer to live in the present," Sebastian replied evenly. "In the present, I control a vast, multinational empire, and you are a washed-up, middle-aged, pitiful excuse for a man, robbing storage facilities of Swiss army knives and spare car parts."

Sebastian caught the slightest twitch of Rossini's left hand, obscured in his pocket.

"You would do well to watch your tone with me, *ragazzo*," he said with a snarl. "Business might be going well now, but you would be nowhere without me. Just a spoiled little kid that ran away from Catholic school."

Sebastian now knew the location of the detonator. Rossini was hiding it in his left pocket and prepared to press it. He needed to distract the mobster for a few minutes to assess the situation.

"Tell me, Gio," he said invitingly, "how would you have handled things differently?"

That did the trick. Rossini sat up straighter. "First of all, you have absolutely no respect for your elders. You take and you take but you give back nothing. Second, this consolidating business – makes no sense to me. With all the lakes and the states and even Canada; I understood New York, but an expansion this large is not sustainable..."

Sebastian tuned him out. As he prattled on, Sebastian considered new possible scenarios. There must be some kind of detonation device in Rossini's pocket, and considering his earlier sweep of the room, Rossini or his men must be wearing the bombs themselves. He was truly surprised at the dedication.

As for the detonator, Sebastian figured since Rossini's hand was in his pocket, consciously holding onto the device, it would only need the click of a button to go off.

If that were the case though, why was he keeping his hand in his pocket the whole time? He could reach in there whenever he wanted; why give himself the discomfort of holding onto it throughout the meeting?

You would do well to watch your tone with me, he had threatened earlier. Perhaps then, the act was already, clandestinely, underway. Perhaps...

"...not to mention, this so-called mafia of yours. Who is this buffoon with you, your consigliere? He looks like he doesn't even know how to handle a gun. And I noticed you have some girlies on your team as well. Bet they don't do you any good. Ha! Women. What do you use them for, mopping up blood and making dinners? When I was in charge, I had some really good men on my team – strong and courageous fellas. You wouldn't know what it's like to have a real army. Let me tell you what those guys could do..."

As Rossini continued, Sebastian reached his conclusion. The detonator was in fact in his pocket and it was already pressed. He had noticed the slight difference in tension between Rossini's right and left arm. He was holding down the button this very moment.

Rossini entered the meeting fully prepared to die. Releasing the button would activate an explosion. Sebastian grit his teeth as he realized the flaw in his plan. As soon as Nick and Lucy fired, killing Rossini, his finger would leave the button and detonate the bomb.

No way around it. The Newspaper was never wrong. Sebastian focused on mitigating the damage, but he had to admit he was touched by Rossini's determination to get rid of him.

"I have to stop you there," he said finally. "I'm an equal opportunity employer. Besides, those ladies could run circles around you on your best day, which is far from today."

"Ha! Very funny," Rossini said. "And this guy?" he gestured to Mike with his right hand.

"My best man," Sebastian affirmed. "Mike, go to the car and get the briefcase from the trunk. Now, if you would."

Confused but reliable, Mike gave a quick nod and exited the room. This wasn't part of the plan, but Sebastian knew he would search the car desperately for a nonexistent briefcase.

"What could you possibly want to bring up here?" Rossini asked, a smug smile creeping onto his lip. "It's too late now for any deals or offerings."

Sebastian pushed his chair back slightly, watching him. "What would drive you to this point, Gio? Why now?"

Rossini shook his head. "You really are a piece of work, Nové, you know that?"

"Oh!" Sebastian exclaimed, as the pieces clicked into place. "This is about Rocco, isn't it? Were you colluding with him in Venice?" He inhaled dramatically. *"Gio!* You should have told me. Now I understand. Without the Mala del Brenta, you really have nothing."

The veins in Rossini's forehead bulged as he reddened with anger. "Rocco should have killed you. I suppose it will have to be me instead, unless you have anything left to say?"

"No," he said, sincerely hoping that Mike was out of the building. "I don't suppose I should kick a *dead horse* when it's down."

The room went dark.

For a split second, Sebastian was overcome with pride that Noa fulfilled his mission after all.

Then, half a heartbeat before three clockwork gun shots rang through the window, he dropped off the chair onto the floor, covered himself with the coat, and flipped the desk ninety degrees, using it to shield himself from the impending—

BOOM!

Although he covered his ears, the blast was deafening. Blinding light enveloped the room for a flash and then disappeared, replaced by crackling flames. The bodies of

Rossini and the two men at his side were engulfed immediately.

The violent explosion cracked the old walls and sent the lights from the ceiling crashing to the floor. The steel desk, which shielded Sebastian from the brunt of the blast, trapped him against the crumbling brick from the force of the detonation.

As the flames viciously spread through the room, Sebastian ignored the ringing in his ears and channeled his strength into pushing the desk away just enough to escape. The open window helped diffuse the smoke, but still his lungs grew heavy and his vision hazed over from the fumes.

Struggling to breathe, he shed the puffy coat, which cushioned his impact against the wall, and crawled out from behind the desk. The fire had spread to the walls, and in his escape, the flames hungrily jumped to his shirt, eating through it and into his flesh.

But there was no time to think about the pain. He could already hear the creaking of the building's foundation. It would not last long.

Covering his mouth and nose from the smoke, he inched his way to the window, looking down the four stories to the alley. He didn't have much of a choice. He climbed over the side, holding onto the pane tightly, and began his descent.

In the back of his mind, Sebastian noted that the Newspaper mentioned nothing of more survivors. Only the five, odd people on the sidewalk, which were undoubtedly his teammates. There was a chance, he reckoned, that he wouldn't survive.

But, with some effort, he made it down to the pavement. He found Mike's getaway car and sped to the Four Seasons, before the adrenaline wore off.

- New York City. Friday, February 21, 2014 -

Noa had spent a good portion of the night in Sebastian's penthouse suite, treating his burns. Despite consistent evidence to the contrary, he couldn't help but feel somewhat responsible.

When the early light of dawn broke through the elegant windows, Noa realized that he had fallen asleep on the bedside chair. He sat up slowly, achingly, and stretched with a quiet yawn.

Sebastian was sound asleep on the bed, atop the blankets, an arm draped over his eyes.

Noa stood as silently as possible and examined his handiwork. He had patched up the burns fairly well, but Sebastian would surely need professional medical attention soon. Noa pulled up part of the blanket from the side of the large bed and covered him with it delicately.

He tip-toed his way to the door, careful not to make a sound, when he suddenly paused in front of the closet. He turned to face the locked safe. This was a perfect chance to investigate.

Wait, investigate?

Noa glanced back at the slumbering Sebastian.

He felt dizzy.

Noa took a hesitant step towards the door, bracing himself against the wall. He had just experienced one of the most stressful events in his life. He had just spent hours tending to the wounds of—who, a criminal?

He was an agent, on a mission to uncover these criminals – to bring them to justice.

And yet he dreaded the prospect of Sebastian dying in that explosion. The visceral panic that paralyzed him when he saw those flames – that was real. As was the relief.

Why? Isn't he just... a criminal?

Noa shook his head, forcefully pushing the thoughts out of his brain. He decided against investigating, considering his own physical state and the fact that Sebastian might wake up at any moment. Instead, he silently left the room and crept back to his own.

Although he was tired and his body ached for rest, he knew he had to contact his boss. He was already late but how could he have anticipated the explosion? If only Sebastian had told them it would happen. How did he know it would, anyway?

Noa mulled over the question as he powered up his computer, logging onto the secure-access frequency chat.

```
[AK |07:30 AM] Hi Agent. Please report on
your status.
[AK| 07:40 AM] Noa? Are you there?
[AK |07:45 AM] Noa please respond
[AK| 08:00 AM] hello?
[NS| 08:33 AM] hi I'm sorry I'm here
[AK| 08:35 AM] Our scheduled time was over
an hour ago
[AK| 08:36 AM] What is the meaning of this?
[NS| 08:37 AM] sorry I know
[AK| 08:37 AM] What's going on? Are you
safe?
[NS| 08:38 AM] I was on a mission with them
[AK| 08:38 AM] What
[NS| 08:39 AM] it was a test to see if I
was loyal, an initiation or something
[NS| 08:39 AM] it was on the news I'll
show you
```

[NS| 08:41 AM] **Sending Attachment: [<u>NYC Building Collapses After Explosion</u> 📎]**
[NS| 08:42 AM] **[File transferred successfully]**
[AK| 08:44 AM] What
[AK| 08:44 AM] **[User has disconnected]**

Noa watched the screen in confusion. His boss ended the conversation so abruptly that he wondered if there was an error. As he tried to troubleshoot the connection, his cell phone rang in his pocket. The display showed a withheld caller ID.

He answered it dubiously. "Hello?"

Agent Koven's voice came through the other end. "Are you alone and in a secure location?"

Noa took this chance to push his computer to the side and lay back on the bed, lazily holding the phone to his ear.

"Oh, hi sir. Yeah, I'm in a hotel room. Isn't it dangerous to use the cellular network?"

"Yes, which is why I'd like to keep this short. But I felt that the text chat was not efficient enough for these purposes." His voice was stern, carrying an authoritative tone even over the phone.

"Okay?" Noa said with some concern.

"You sent me an article about an explosion in downtown NYC last night. You were involved in this? Are you hurt? Tell me what happened."

"I was sort of involved." Noa replayed the events past 24 hours in his mind. "They had set up a meeting with some mobster guy, and I was in a building across the street. I had to turn off the lights at a precise moment, but then the building exploded. Apparently, the guy was packing bombs." He paused. "I wasn't really injured. Just a little sore."

Koven stayed silent for a few moments. "You placed yourself in a dangerous situation, agent. You could have been hurt or killed." There was another short break. "I will put in a request immediately to have you pulled from the case."

"What?!" Noa jolted up into a sitting position, nearly dropping the cell phone. "No! Sir, with all due respect, you can't do that! I worked so hard to get this far and now they trust me. Truly trust me."

"This mission is not more important than your life."

Noa's heart sank. He hadn't considered this outcome.

"Please," he begged, "you have to let me stay on this case. I don't think I'll need to participate in any more missions, and the investigation will progress a lot smoother now."

Noa heard a sigh. "Are you any closer to determining how they get the inside scoop on stock prices?"

"Yes, I am," he lied.

"And?"

"Well," Noa bit his lip. Suddenly, he had a revelation. "I believe they may be getting more prognostic information than just stocks. The Boss knew the explosion would happen before it did. As if he has a fortune teller or something."

"A fortune teller?" His boss didn't sound convinced. "Anything else?"

Noa wracked his tired brain for information. "I learned more about the members of the team, sir. For example, one of the women, the Asian one, has a military background. She seems to be a highly skilled assassin."

"Interesting," Koven said, typing something on his end. "Is there anything peculiar about her?"

"Peculiar?" Noa asked. He thought about Lucy, feeling an increasingly dreadful sense of guilt as he did so. "She's strong, and very quiet. Oh, and she's always wearing a scarf, I guess."

More typing over the phone. "Incredible," came the reply. "Yes, she is a known fugitive. Be wary of her, Noa. She is ruthless and extremely dangerous; try not to go near her if you can. Did you learn anything else?"

Noa felt a traitorous chill run down his spine. He swallowed hard, wondering what Lucy must have done in her past to warrant such a caution from his boss – and how he could have deduced her identity so quickly.

"Nothing really remarkable about the rest of them," he said. "But now that I'm officially part of the team, I can find out much more."

Koven made a slight noise of approval. "You think you can speed matters up from this point?"

"Yes, absolutely." Noa tried to contain the nerves in his voice. "Leave it to me sir, I won't let you down. Please don't take me off the case."

"Just know that you're on thin ice, Noa. I'll be keeping a close eye on you. You're my responsibility."

"Understood, sir. Will that be all?"

The voice on the other end sighed again. "Yes. Keep up the good work. And for god's sake, stay safe."

With a click, the line went dead. Noa unclenched the whitened hand that was holding his cell phone and fell back down onto the bed.

His chest ached. Partially from the blast and partially from an unknown source. The fear of failing his mission. The fear of losing his new f—

He covered his face with the pillow and shouted into it.

He reminded himself why he was here. These people were evil! The Niagara Co. was manipulating the very fabric of the free market. They were participating in international drug and arms trades, not to mention *murder*.

On top of that, Noa figured the members must have criminal pasts. Lucy, it would seem, was on the top of some very clandestine lists. Nick brought in weapons and ammunition and seemed apt at using them.

As for Elli and Mike, well, they must have done something bad to find themselves on this team, right?

Noa removed the pillow.

He would uncover the truth, no matter what.

FOUR
DANGER

- Toronto. Friday, February 21, 2014 -

Beyond the expansive windows of Director Colson's south side office, cloudy grey skies met and vanished into a grey, watery horizon. She placed her oversized mug down with an audible *thud* and removed her heeled shoes off the desk when her door slid open.

"Alex! I wasn't expecting you this early. Aren't you missing your weekly game with Miriam?" She beckoned him inside.

"Morning, ma'am," Agent Koven entered the office, shutting the door behind him. "Yes, but it's fine. I always lose anyway."

"Well, don't dawdle over there. Come, sit. I have some time before the national forum," she said. "The rolling twelve trends are showing a net decrease in organized crime reported along the border, especially around the lakes. Either they're getting better at hiding from us or they're gearing up for something big. Regardless, we need a break in this Niagara case."

Koven sat in one of the chairs across from her desk with some hesitation. "Right. That is partially the reason for my visit," he said. "I like your coffee mug," he added, easing the tension.

Colson chuckled, wrapping her hands around it. "A gift from my daughter. Clever, right? *My job is top secret – even I don't know what I'm doing.* I think she gets upset that I don't tell her anything."

"Understandable," he said. "How old is your daughter?"

The director sighed. "Thirteen. You know anything about teenagers? She's been begging me for Justin Bieber tickets. I just don't get the appeal."

Koven shook his head. "Afraid not. Closest connection I have to a teenager is probably Agent Sinclair and I doubt he's into that kind of music."

"How is little Red anyway?" she asked. "Working the Niagara case, right?"

"That's what I'd like to discuss, ma'am," Koven said with an inhale. "He seems to be getting closer to uncovering details about the inner operations of the Niagara Co., but I believe he might be putting himself in significant danger."

Colson raised a brow. "Well, yes, Alex. He chose to go undercover to infiltrate a known criminal syndicate. Did you think he was going camping?"

"No ma'am, but originally we thought he had simply found a subdivision of Niagara Co., and that the members would be run-of-the-mill mobsters," he said. "However, it would appear that Noa managed to get involved with the inner circle. And one of the insiders might be NL-9009."

"NL-9009?" The director leaned in. "You can't be serious, Alex. If anyone even hears you say that—"

"I have good reason to believe it's her," Koven asserted, lowering his voice. "Ma'am, I've been tracking the NL-9000 project since I got the clearance. Noa's description and the geographic location lines up."

Colson sat back, crossing her arms. "That is a concern."

A brief silence passed between them as the director rested her head against the chair, studying the ceiling tiles in concentration.

"What do you suggest?" he asked after some time.

"Sinclair doesn't have clearance on the NL-9000, right?"

"No, it's blacklisted. Even with his deep web hacking, there isn't any information about it anywhere online," Koven confirmed.

"Okay." She tapped a finger against her arm. "I agree that it's a dangerous situation. But, assuming NL-9009 is working with Niagara Co., she is unlikely to pose an immediate threat as long as he doesn't blow his cover. Exposing the insider trading is Sinclair's primary objective. That being said, if you perceive his safety to be in jeopardy, you can pull him out."

Koven nodded, standing from the chair. "Understood, ma'am. I'll keep a close eye on him."

"Good. Oh, by the way, I looked into Sinclair after your note a couple weeks back," she said, opening her deskside drawer. "I should have told you sooner. When they sent him, that institution also sent over some transfer documents." She placed a manila folder in front of her.

Koven glanced at the label. "Why is it dated November 15th?"

"I don't know," she shrugged. "But, regarding those burns you mentioned, his file says he lost both parents in a house fire when he was a child. That might explain the scars. And I guess this school doubles as an orphanage."

"Hm," Koven skimmed through the files, consisting of

handwritten notes and some newspaper clippings. "Lee said the injuries looked deliberate," he added under his breath.

"You can take those, if you want. It's also on our database now, since they sent it over," Colson said, turning her attention elsewhere. "Good luck finding out any information about that school though, it's off the grid."

"I see. Thank you, ma'am." he took the folder, going to the door.

Director Colson hit the table suddenly. "Oh! One more thing, Alex."

He stopped, hand on the handle.

"I heard through my grapevine that the SFPD has an informant that might have a lead on a Niagara Co. member," she said. "I didn't tell them about our operation, of course."

"Should I inform Noa?" Koven asked.

"No," she said. "Best he remains focused on his task. If you ask me, I doubt they'll succeed – but we might learn something from it with our insider."

"Yes, ma'am."

- New York City. Friday, February 21, 2014 -

Unable to eat, sleep, or even smoke, Noa stared at his cellphone screen with tired eyes, mindlessly sliding colored blocks into place. Upon clearing yet another game of Tetris, he flung the device across the mattress and lazily rolled off the bed.

He needed more information, but where to begin? Cooped up in the hotel room, he fixated on Agent Koven's warning about Lucy, but his internet research yielded no results. Noa spent all morning scouring the deep web in vain – which meant he needed to get back to his government-issued computer for drastic measures.

He glanced out the window, squinting from the light of the winter sun. Niagara was over six hours away by car, but he would have to find a ride sooner or later because the helicopter in which they arrived probably wouldn't fly him alone.

Noa put his phone in his pocket and packed up his few belongings, leaving the hotel room. He crept down the hallway quietly, listening for familiar voices from behind the penthouse doors.

He lingered temporarily by Sebastian's room. Silence.

With a shaky exhale, Noa approached the elevator, glanced over his shoulder and pressed the button to descend.

"Hey, kiddo! You're lookin' much better today."

Noa staggered back as the elevator doors slid open. Mike stepped out, his arms full with fast food takeout bags.

"Mind helping me out with these?"

"Sure," Noa grabbed a couple items, moving out of his way.

Mike eyed the boy's backpack. "You headed somewhere?"

Noa weighed the benefits of lying and decided against it. "Just home," he said quietly.

"Oh! Why don't you catch a ride with us, then?" Mike said, stopping in front of a hotel room adjacent to his own. "Me and Luce were just going to have lunch and get goin'."

"What about the rest of the team?"

Mike knocked on the door nine times, with pauses in between certain knocks. "They're stickin' around a bit longer. Elli's got something to take care of on Wall Street and Nick will take the boss back when he wakes up. We might as well head back, though. NYC's too crowded for Lucy anyway!"

"Right," Noa muttered as the door unlocked and slowly creaked open.

"Can the newbie join us?" Mike asked, grinning at Lucy. "He'll sit in the back."

Lucy nodded once, letting them through. Noa noted the scarf around her neck, even indoors, but focused his attention elsewhere.

He placed the takeout on the hotel table and sat on the edge of the bed, watching Mike and Lucy set up the rest of the food. His foot touched something under the bed – some kind of long luggage. Noa leaned over upside down for a better look.

Mike chuckled with a mouthful of fries. "I think he wants to see your toys, Luce."

Noa snapped back up, coming face-to-face with Lucy's steely eyes. He hadn't heard her move to stand right in front of him.

"S-sorry," he said, inching back on the bed.

Without a word, Lucy kneeled down and retrieved a long, pale green bag from underneath the bed. It had a handle and a few zippers all the way along the perimeter. She motioned to it with an open palm.

Noa looked to the bag, then to the silent woman, then back to bag.

Hesitantly, he climbed off the bed and crouched in front of the luggage, carefully unzipping it. Once unfastened, with a slight pause, Noa flipped open the top.

"Nice, right?" Mike said, taking a bite out of a burger.

Noa nodded nervously, staring at the military grade sniper rifle resting within its case. *Did she use this in Italy as well?* The Venetian mobster found in Murano's canals died from a single shot to the head. Sniped from a distance.

"Ah, jeez, I'm being so rude," Mike said suddenly. "I didn't even offer you Wendy's! D'you want some, kiddo?"

Noa zipped up the bag, keeping his gaze down. "No, thanks. I'm good."

Back in his Niagara Falls apartment, Noa triple checked the locks on his door and then scrambled to start up his work computer.

The six-and-a-half-hour drive from New York City felt even longer as Noa's imagination conjured up a hypothetical criminal background for Lucy. At the very least, it was clear that she was dangerous, despite Mike's nonchalance around her. No – nonchalance is not the right way to describe it. Lovestruck was more like it.

Noa poured over government files, searching for any trace mentions for a person of interest matching Lucy's description. As the day rolled into evening and his eyes grew weary, he set up an automated bot to continue the search while he made coffee and pulled up his own file on the Niagara Co.

Lucy was a wild card. Quiet but lethal. Something about her scarf tipped off his boss – maybe she had a marking or a tattoo on her neck? Noa scribbled some thoughts in his notebook, pausing when a beep signaled the end of his program's auto-search.

He peered at the screen over the steam of the coffee and furrowed his brows. Nothing.

"You don't say?" He muttered to himself, sliding in

front of the laptop. "Either you're a ghost or I have insufficient clearance."

Noa felt around under his mattress for the 11-marked cube, connecting it to the computer. After playing around with the code for a while, he brought up a mirrored version of Agent Koven's login credentials, cursing under his breath that he changed them since Noa's initial hack.

He ran a password cracker in the background while pacing the floor.

Why did he even want to know? Did this information matter? Clearly, his superiors already knew more about Lucy than he did. Maybe that's what bothered him. Shouldn't they have shared the full picture? Doesn't he deserve to know the truth of the situation?

Ping.

Noa forced down the rest of his coffee and sat at the computer. He opened the government classified database, fingers hovering over the keys. Searching for keywords would be risky. The searched tags are saved to the user, and Koven would notice something was off.

Instead, Noa skimmed the agent's history for a Lucy-related term. He recognized most of the search words – related to national threats or various border crime – but one stood out as unfamiliar: Project NL-9000.

Cursor over the article name, he checked the time. He had to be careful, since he had remote access to Koven's computer. If the agent was online at the same time, he would notice. But, considering it was past 8:00 on a Friday night, Noa took a breath and clicked.

FIVE
[REDACTED]

Project NL-9000

The data provided within this document is restricted to SECURITY LEVEL 4 (TOP SECRET). Please note that accessing this file without proper authorization will result in disciplinary action, up to and including termination of employment.

If you wish to continue, select the project-specific iteration.

~~[NL-9001]~~ ERROR//: file corrupted
~~[NL-9002]~~ ERROR//: file corrupted
~~[NL-9003]~~ ERROR//: file corrupted
~~[NL-9004]~~ ERROR//: file corrupted
~~[NL-9005]~~ ERROR//: file corrupted
~~[NL-9006]~~ ERROR//: file corrupted
~~[NL-9007]~~ ERROR//: file corrupted
~~[NL-9008]~~ ERROR//: file corrupted

THE HELL'S HALF ACRE TRADE 49

[NL-9009]

> [NL-9009]
Displaying: NL-9009, Clearance Level 4
File No.: AS2D89

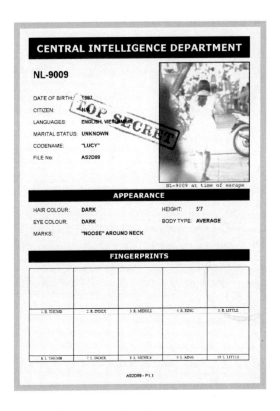

Status: Subject at large.
NOTE: Under special order of Director ▇▇▇▇, Addendum 009-d is attached to the end of the file for subject NL-9009.
Description: NL-9009 (Codename "LUCY") is the ninth and only surviving subject of Project NL-9000.

NL-9009 is a Vietnamese female, recovered from an impoverished neighborhood in the village of ██████, together with subject's sister (NL-9008), both of whom were deemed suitable hosts for NANO LAQUEUS.
NANO LAQUEUS (Project NL-9000) was established on ████ ██,2011, as a joint initiative between the United States and German militaries. NANO LAQUEUS (*lit.* microscopic noose) combines nanotechnology with enhanced combat techniques to ~~create the ultimate human weapon.~~ [**Addendum 009-a:** Following the events of ██-██-2012, Project NL-9000 has been suspended indefinitely by Director ██████.]

Upon arrival to the NANO LAQUEUS facility and full amnesticization, NL-9009 and subject's sister were deemed suitable hosts for the Neuron-Operated Orbital Synthetic Energy device (Codename "NOOSE") and both underwent the operation.

To function, the NOOSE nanobots must gain access to the host's arterial blood and brain. At full capacity, the NOOSE grants the subject an incomparable immune system and metabolism. On average, NOOSE nanobots can arrive at the site of a wound and close it 230% faster than the average leukocyte. Additionally, muscle development is rapidly increased, allowing the host to achieve superhuman strength.

The NOOSE is surgically implanted in the neck, just below the thyroid cartilage. Due to the post-surgical scarring, the implant resembles a ligature mark such as that of a noose.

NOOSE fusion was not successful in most cases.

Addendum 009-b: Current status of NL-9000 subjects

NL-9001 "LUCKY" (deceased ■-■-2011): Expired during NOOSE fusion surgery.
NL-9002 "LEAH" (deceased ■-■-2011): Expired during NOOSE fusion surgery.
NL-9003 "LISA" (deceased ■-■-2011): Self-terminated following a prolonged period of distress post NOOSE fusion surgery.
NL-9004 "LOUIS" (deceased ■-■-2012): Killed during an escape attempt from NANO LAQUEUS facility.
NL-9005 "LEO", **NL-9006 "LOGAN"** & **NL-9007 "LEXI"** (deceased ■-■-2012): See addendum 009-d for description of events, which resulted in numerous casualties, including three NL subjects.
NL-9008 "LILY" (deceased ■-■-2012): Self-terminated.
NL-9009 "LUCY": As of ■-■-2012, NL-9009 has escaped and remains at large. Finding and containing NL-9009 is a top priority.

Of the nine NANO LAQUEUS subjects, NL-9009 was among five that made it to combat testing. Tests included various life-threatening injuries to measure the extent of the NOOSE's strength and regenerative abilities.

NL-9009 successfully completed training, excelling in military exercises and surviving multiple knife & bullet wounds, landmines, immolation, and partial amputation. NL-9009 specialized both in long-range and tactical combat.

On ■-■-2012, NL-9005 ("LEO"), NL-9006 ("LOGAN"), NL-9007 ("LEXI") and NL-9009 ("LUCY") were loaned to the ■ Task Force for military exercises and front-line battle. NANO LAQUEUS regularly checked-in on the status of the subjects to record the results, potential side effects and overall conditions of the NOOSE.

Four months later, on ■-■-2012, Dr. ■, head supervisor of NANO LAQUEUS research, answered an unscheduled call at 11:19 PM from General ■ of ■ Task Force.

Addendum 009-c: Transcript of call made by General ■

<Begin Call>

General ▮: *Garbled* [EXPLETIVE REDACTED], doc. Are you there? Jesus Christ. Is someone there?

Dr. ▮: Hello? Jack, is that you?

General ▮: Thank God! Listen doc, [EXPLETIVE REDACTED] has hit the fan over here — you have to shut it down. Shut it all down.

Dr. ▮: Slow down, Jack! I can barely hear you over all that — what is that? Screaming? What's going on?

General ▮: *Static, garbled.* —WENT INSANE! Just DISMEMBERED them; all of them! So SHUT IT DOWN!

Dr. ▮: Wait, what? You're cutting out. Did you say dismembered?

General ▮: Christ, she's here. *Silence; footsteps.* Stop, please, don't do this, Luce—

Dr. ▮: Hello? Jack? General, are you there? General?

General ▮: *Silence; receding footsteps.*

Dr. ▮: [EXPLETIVE REDACTED].

<End Call>

An investigation into the events at the ▮ Task Force military base on ▮-▮-2012 (see: **Addendum 009-d**) lead to the immediate closure and disbandment of NANO LAQUEUS, including termination of all Project NL-9000 employees under the strictest clearance.

Addendum 009-d: The events of ██-██-2012

On ██-██-2012, three days prior to NL-9009's destructive rampage and subsequent escape, a stray round dispatched by a soldier in training struck the subject's neck. The bullet did not hit any vital areas; however, it did graze the left-most side of the NOOSE and damage it slightly.

NL-9009 immediately lost consciousness and was transferred to a medical tent for monitoring. The wounds with which NL-9009 had been inflicted that day slowed in healing, and the subject remained under observation.

After 24 hours, NL-9009 regained consciousness but was unable to move. The regenerative properties of the NOOSE had not been restored, so the subject stayed in the medical tent.

According to the witness statement provided by Nurse ██-██, one of the only survivors of the attack, on the second night of NL-9009's immobilization, twelve male soldiers from the ████ Task Force combat unit forcibly gained access to the medical tent and [DATA EXPUNGED].

FURTHER INFORMATION ON NL-9009 IS CLASSIFIED LEVEL 5 (DIRECTOR). INSUFFICIENT SECURITY CLEARANCE.

Unease growing in the pit of his stomach, Noa exhaled a breath he didn't realize he was holding as he reached the end of the document. The details lined up. He was sure this was Lucy after all. But he was not at all comforted by the revelation.

Inching away from the monitor, he instead felt as though he intruded by discovering this personal information without permission. Did the rest of her team even know this? Would she tell them? And what would happen if he revealed her location to US officials?

Noa stared at the onscreen words, the [DATA EXPUNGED] mockingly blurring in his vision. Director Colson likely knew the whole story – or at least, had the clearance to find out. Either way, dealing with Lucy was not his objective. He just needed to stay out of her way.

Closing the file and special clearance database, he returned Agent Koven's desktop to the way it was before. A minimized PDF caught Noa's eye just as he was about to relinquish remote access and he hovered the cursor over the Adobe icon.

A tendril of panic seized his chest.

Cambridgeshire house fire that killed two linked to electrical fault (December 19, 2001)

Thirty-three-year-old and twenty-seven-year-old couple found dead at scene in Eynesbury, their four-year old son seriously injured.

. . .

Noa ripped out the connection cable and slammed the laptop closed with enough force to shake the table. His heart felt like a fist pounding the inside of his chest, hammering against his ribcage.

"No, no, no," he breathed, sliding off the bed and sinking to his knees onto the floor.

"No," the boy repeated, struggling to maintain his vision. "Why does he have that?"

Noa shut his eyes, blocking out the terror creeping up from the corners of his memory.

SIX
INTERROGATORIO

- Niagara Falls. Saturday, February 22, 2014 - 10:04 AM

Waking with a jolt, Noa realized he had fallen asleep on the floor. His stomach grumbled with frustration and his neck ached from the awkward angle of his slumber.

Groaning, he got up slowly. It was past 10:00 am already, so he reluctantly dragged himself into a hot shower – which helped with the soreness, somewhat – and changed, tossing his debris and dirt-covered clothes from the explosion in the corner of the room.

After rummaging around the kitchen for something resembling breakfast, Noa hid the investigation notes and government laptop under his mattress and unenthusiastically made his way towards the Polar Parlor.

The bells on the door jingled merrily as he entered, and Elli stiffened behind the frosted white and purple counter. She hastily hid something round behind her back and stuffed a small bag in her apron pocket.

"What are you doing here, sugar? Didn't you get my text?"

Confused, Noa reached into his pocket, pulling the cellphone out. "Sorry, I must've missed it..."

In capital letters, a message from Elli dominated his lock screen: 'DO NOT COME TO THE PARLOR UNTIL 3PM!!!! (ᴜ‿ᴜ✿)' He shook his head shamefully, apologizing again.

"It's fine, it's fine," Elli said, "no harm done. Are you okay? You're paler than usual, hon'. Did you eat?"

Noa focused on a crack in the wooden floorboards, nodding quickly. "Yeah, all good. So, I'm not working today, then?"

"Nope," Elli gestured him out with the hand that was not hidden behind her back. "Now go on, shoo! You look like you need a day off."

With another nod, Noa turned back to the door which had just opened with a jingle to a couple of customers. Under her breath, Noa thought he heard Elli grumble '— thought I flipped that stupid Open sign to Closed,' before switching to her usual friendly demeanor.

"Welcome! What can I get you folks?" she asked the pair, a mother and her small son, while stuffing whatever she was hiding under the counter.

"What do you want, Freddy?" the woman asked, inspecting the menu.

The young boy ran up to the counter, standing on his tip toes. He pointed to a vaguely bear-shaped machine in the corner, "Wha'sat?"

"Oh, this doohicky?" Elli smiled at Noa, who was still loitering by the door. "Allow me to introduce the PecanBot 2.0! It's an ice cream robot. Do you want to see it in action, Freddy?" she retrieved a remote from her apron, showing it to the boy.

The child hopped up and down, "Yeah!"

"Okay, it only does a few flavors for now, though," Elli said. "Do you want to try Chocolate Falls or Caribou Tracks?"

"Chocolate!" he shouted, eagerly watching the machine.

"You got it! Hold onto your hats and mittens," Elli started up the second iteration of the PecanBot, which sprang to life with a soft hum. More controlled and less noisy than the prototype, the ice cream machine pumped a scoop of chocolate into a cone and gently placed it into a slot on a conveyor belt, that carried the treat to its awaiting consumer.

The boy watched with wonder, pulling on his mother's coat. "Wow, look! Robot!"

Elli beamed. "Isn't it so cool?"

The boy's mother opened her mouth to reply but was interrupted by the Staff Only door swinging open with an audible bang as it smashed against the wall.

You could hear a pin drop in the Parlor as Sebastian entered in a rage.

"Where is Noa?" He demanded, grabbing Elli by the arm.

Noa tensed, subconsciously pressing himself against the wall.

"The hell, Bassie?" Elli yanked her arm free, crossing both across her chest. "You're scaring the customers!"

He glanced at them. The young boy hid behind his mother's legs, and she was glaring at Sebastian furiously. In the far end of the Polar Parlor, he spotted a familiar redhead, frozen to the floor.

Sebastian looked away and pinched the bridge of his nose as he closed his eyes. "I don't care. They can piss off."

The mother scoffed in outrage. "Some customer

service!" She took her son's hand and pulled him to the door.

"Please, at least take the ice cream," Elli exclaimed, but it was too late. The sad boy's face disappeared behind the glass of the Parlor's doors with a sardonic jingle.

Elli shook her head with a huff, "See what you've done! Was that really necessary— whoa, Bassie. What- what happened to you?"

Stepping back, Elli realized she hadn't seen him since before the mission. Beneath an open dress shirt, his chest was covered in gauze bandages. Smaller, traveling burns spread like lightening to his stomach and shoulders, uncovered.

"Just a flesh wound," he replied tiredly. Turning to face Noa again, his tone darkened. "You. My office." Then, without pause, he left through the employee door just as abruptly as he arrived.

Alone with Elli in the ghostly stillness of an empty Polar Parlor, Noa seriously regretted coming in today. He remained glued to the wall, unwilling to move.

"Noa, hon'," Elli said softly. "Did you do something?"

He desperately hoped not. At least, not anything overt. "I don't think so," he mumbled.

Elli tucked a lock of hair behind her ear, removing the abandoned cone of Chocolate Falls ice cream from Pecan-Bot's conveyor belt. "He rarely loses it like that," she said. "Bassie is a bit of a drama queen, but not when it comes to hissy fits."

"Do you think it's my fault?" Noa asked nervously.

"I'm sure it'll be fine, sugar," she said. "But go find out, because I don't want him storming in here like that again. Here, take this," she handed him the ice cream. "He likes chocolate."

Noa peeled himself off the wall, leaving his coat by the front and taking the cone, hesitantly going to the back door. "Okay. Wish me luck."

Elli smiled, "Just tell him that if anything happens to you, he'll have to answer to me. And don't come back here until 3:00, got it?"

Noa nodded with a small smile, "Got it."

"Oh, actually," she added quickly, "if you're seeing Bassie anyway, can you give him an update for me? Tell him that thirty-four—" she cut herself off with a hum. "Thirty-four horses dropped dead in Minnesota."

"Huh?" Noa raised a brow. "Why... why would he care about that?"

Elli shrugged, returning to the conveyor belt. "Thanks for passing it on! See you at 3:00, hon'."

"Right," Noa said, mostly to himself. "See you."

Keeping a hand under the ice cream to catch any melting droplets, he made his way to the hidden elevator and descended to the 14th floor beneath the ground. He didn't know what to expect when he reached Sebastian's office, but he was quite sure he hadn't done anything to warrant suspicion. At least, that's what he hoped.

He knocked at the door.

After a few moments of silence, Noa pressed his ear to the entrance. "Um, hello? It's me. Can I come in?"

Finally, the door unlocked and opened slowly on its own. Noa peered inside cautiously before stepping in.

Sebastian sat in the chair at his desk, facing the wall.

Noa dabbed at a growing chocolate stain on the cuff of his sweater sleeve, keeping his head down. "You know, I think this office would be much nicer above ground, with some windows. Then you wouldn't have to stare at walls and stuff."

He slapped himself mentally for saying something so stupid.

Though he was fixated on the floor, Noa could practically sense Sebastian's hard gaze.

An eternity passed before Sebastian stood. "Why did you leave yesterday morning?"

The agent blinked, looking up at last. "Pardon?"

Sebastian sighed with irritation. "Yesterday morning. You left me alone and then proceeded to leave New York entirely. Why would you do that?"

Oh no. He's suspicious of me, thought Noa. He couldn't say that he left in a hurry to contact his boss about the mission. And then had to return to his government-issued laptop to investigate further.

Sebastian made an attempt to cross his arms but immediately thought better of it. "So? What was so important that you decided to leave your boss in such a condition?"

Noa fidgeted uncomfortably, "I had to get back home to... feed my... fish."

What the hell am I saying? Noa held his breath, cursing himself for such a dumb excuse. He couldn't think clearly in Sebastian's presence to muster up a believable reason.

Sebastian watched him. "To feed your *fish*? You had to leave at the crack of dawn for that?"

Too late to escape the sinkhole beneath his feet. Noa committed. "Well, yes sir. It's a six-and-a-half-hour drive. And I couldn't feed them since we left on the mission. So, I had to hurry, especially since Flipper had been sick lately."

"You have fish," Sebastian repeated. "What kind of fish are they? I don't remember seeing them at your place."

It had occurred to Noa then that if he kept up this lie, the Niagara Co.'s don would want to see these non-existent fish. He lowered his voice to a mournful whisper.

"They *used* to be goldfish. I kept them in my bedroom. Sir."

"*Used* to be?"

"They died," Noa said sorrowfully, meeting Sebastian's gaze. "Yesterday, when I went to feed them, I guess they got sicker or too hungry."

There was a long silence. Noa didn't dare say anything more.

Sebastian drew in a deep breath. "Alright. So, you had fish. And you left early to feed them, but they had already died?"

Noa just nodded solemnly, melting chocolate ice cream dripping down his hand.

"I see," he said. "I suppose there is only one thing to be done then."

Noa readied himself for the worst. "Yes?"

In a striking change of demeanor, Sebastian pulled his coat out of the office closet. "Get you some new fish, obviously. Since they perished as a result of my negligence."

"I... beg your pardon?" Noa stammered.

"Come on then," he said, grabbing the cone from Noa and striding out the door. "Let's go."

Two things surprised Noa. The first was the ease with which Sebastian believed his fishy fib. The reason for this was either a) Noa was a much more convincing liar than he originally thought, or b) Sebastian was in some kind of weakened mental state. Or an unknown c) factor. He didn't ponder this for long however, because he was soon surprised by the second thing.

Sebastian's idea of replacing Noa's bowl of imaginary

goldfish was to buy an aquarium. A huge, wall-mounted fish-tank. Noa protested, noting that it wouldn't even fit in his room. And, considering he didn't actually know how to care for fish, he felt overwhelmed by the sudden responsibility.

Sebastian just brushed him off, preoccupied with the task of picking out a variety of tropical fish.

After Sebastian had paid for the aquarium supplies and the fish, Noa insisted that he at least pay for one miniature treasure chest for the aquarium's floor. He ran back to the cashier to buy the decoration while Sebastian went to unload the rest of the purchases.

He paid for the treasure chest and left the store, continuously wondering how he was at a pet shop buying fish with a highly wanted criminal.

As he approached the car, he noticed Sebastian speaking on the phone.

"—just get 200 of the AMK-75s, up to AMK-100 if they have it. What? No, don't get the AR-15. Are you mad?"

Noting by the subject of guns, Noa figured that he was likely talking to Nick. He crept up closer.

"Listen, the AR-15 uses a direct impingement system – basically, 'shit where you eat.' Even a hedgehog understands that. Don't get those." Sebastian took the little treasure chest from Noa and tossed it in with other supplies in the trunk.

Noa wondered what an impingement system was. Also, why would a hedgehog know that? If that was an idiom, Noa never heard of it.

"Call me when it's done, Nick." Sebastian opened the passenger door for Noa and got in the car himself.

When he hung up, Noa asked, "Are those guns you were talking about?"

"Yes," Sebastian replied, starting the car. "Nick is negotiating a purchase right now."

Noa kept his gaze forward, watching the cars in front of them. "What else do you guys trade in?"

Sebastian smiled subtly. "What else do you think, Noa?"

It was a trap, and he knew it. Noa mustered up courage, maintaining an oblivious air. "Drugs?"

"Yes. What else?"

"Organs?"

Sebastian grimaced. "No."

"Assassinations?"

"No," Sebastian said firmly. "Death is a last resort."

Noa took the plunge. "Information?"

From the corner of his eye, Sebastian glanced at his passenger. "Information? What do you mean by that?"

Noa stared forward blankly, chewing on the inside of his mouth. "Um, I don't know. Like underground intel on stuff?"

"Intel on *what*, Noa?"

He was going to make him say it. "The stock market, maybe? I mean, Mike mentioned Elli went to Wall Street yesterday and something about stocks," he said, completely lying about the second part.

Sebastian let out an unamused chuckle. "Mike would. A man should never miss an opportunity to keep his mouth shut."

"So, you *do* sell information?" Noa asked hopefully, gaining confidence. "How do you get it in advance? Do you have moles on Wall Street?"

"You're asking a lot of questions above your pay grade, Noa," Sebastian said in a warning tone.

Dejected, Noa decided it was best to cease his line of

questioning for now. "Sorry," he said. "Oh, before I forget, Elli told me to tell you something about dead horses."

"Did she?" Sebastian pulled up to Noa's apartment complex. "What did she say?"

"I don't really get it. She said 34 horses died in Minnesota. What does that mean?"

The car slowed to a stop. "That is also above your pay grade, I'm afraid. But thank you for the update."

Inwardly frustrated, Noa led Sebastian upstairs to his apartment and unlocked the door.

"Still a mess," Sebastian said as he stepped inside. "Are those your clothes from the blast on the floor?"

Noa reddened, snatching up the dirty laundry. "M-maybe. I didn't have time to clean."

Sebastian turned to him. "Noa, perhaps these conditions were not suitable for your aquatic friends from the beginning." He looked around the room. "And anyway, it seems you were right; the tank is definitely not going to fit here."

"Definitely not," Noa said, carefully eyeing the part of his mattress under which his laptop was hidden. "So, what now?"

Sebastian stroked his chin. "Hm. I guess the Polar Parlor is getting an upgrade."

- Port Stanley. Saturday, February 22, 2014 - Same time

Nick slid his phone back into his pocket with a shrug. "He said absolutely no AR-15s."

"Damn it," Mike exclaimed, "I already put in an order for 100 next month!"

"Well, you're gonna have to be that one to tell him that. And he might call you a hedgehog, or whatever."

Nick and Mike were idling in the *Aurora III* in Lake Erie at the harbor of a small municipality in Ontario, waiting for a shipment of weapons to arrive.

A few months after recruiting Nick, Sebastian made use his ties to the Californian mafia. Hailing from San Francisco and related to the Sicilian Cosa Nostra, Nick had many contacts on the West Coast, despite the fallout that led to his encounter with Niagara Co.

Nick refused to go back to California for any reason, so all the shipments had to cross many borders in clandestine vehicles.

It was an expensive method of transport, but Nick's negotiating prowess with the West Coast was worth the sacrifice. And Sebastian was well aware that in addition to the San Francisco police department's search for Nick, it was also much too painful for him to step onto the soil of his old home to face the reminders of his ex-wife and family.

So, instead of flying Nick out to California, the shipments would travel north from California through Nevada and Idaho, and then head East through the Canadian prairies. Upon reaching Ontario, the merchandise would be sent to the port of Lake Erie (which was less guarded than Lake Ontario) and picked up by the *Aurora*, transported by boat to Niagara Falls.

The two of them had done these trades countless times, and only encountered problems once, when the courier demanded a cut of the profits or he'd talk. Nick dealt with him swiftly.

Mike leaned against the bow of the yacht and yawned. "Ugh, they're late. I need to get back soon to help Elli prep for this afternoon."

Nick checked his watch. "I wonder what the holdup is. Hope they didn't get caught along the way."

After a few more minutes, an unmarked van pulled up to the dock.

"Fuckin' finally," Nick said. "You have the new orders ready?"

"Yeah," Mike handed him the papers. "Maybe we can get the AR-15s off the supply chain, if it's not too late."

"We'll see." Nick said, eyeing the vehicle.

The windows were tinted, for security, and the doors had number pad locks instead of key locks. The truck popped open with a click, revealing their merchandise.

"It's about fuckin' time," Nick grumbled.

The driver side door creaked open as the courier stepped out. Nick froze, eyes wide.

"...Angelina?"

- Niagara Falls. Saturday, February 22, 2014 - 12:15PM

"Are you *kidding me*?" Elli shouted in exasperation. "Sugar, bless your heart, but what part of *don't come back until 3:00* did you not get through your ginger little head?"

Noa had just stepped through the jingling doors of the Parlor carrying aquarium supplies and walked straight into an ambush by Elli, who blocked his path with her body.

"I— but Sebastian said—"

"What are you doing here?" She grabbed a small mesh net from his hands. "What is all this stuff?"

Sebastian pushed open the doors with a dolly, atop which rested the disassembled parts of a giant fish tank. "Surprise! Time for another upgrade."

"Another *what?*" Elli seethed, glaring at him. "Did you have to do this *today*? Does no one read my texts?"

Sebastian looked around the Parlor. "Are we intruding on something?"

Elli fumed. "If you weren't burnt to a crisp, I'd beat you up. Scaring my customers; ruining my plans. Why are you out and about anyway? Go home!"

Sebastian calmly retrieved a clear bag of water from a box on the dolly, holding it out to Elli. "Don't you want to meet this guy?" Inside, a small black fish, with a fluttering skirt fin and a long tail swam in circles around its perimeter.

"Oh," Elli's features noticeably softened. "Aw, how precious." She took the bag carefully, cooing at the fish inside. "Hi, little fishy! You look like a tiny ghost. I'll name you Casper."

Sebastian winked at Noa. "Crisis averted."

"I'm still mad," Elli called over her shoulder, returning to the counter and hiding various items haphazardly behind it. "And where in the world is Mike? He was supposed to help me."

Sebastian unloaded the cart, setting the aquarium materials on the floor. "Him and Nick should be here soon. Nick called earlier to say the courier was running late."

"Guess this upgrade takes full priority. What got into you, Bassie?" Elli said. "Did the doctor check your head?" When he just laughed in response, she doubled down. "I'm not joking! If you were in that blast to get burned so badly... Are those scars going to be permanent?"

"Let's change the subject, shall we?" Sebastian handed Noa the treasure chest he picked out. "Which wall would be best?"

Changing the subject on his behalf, the doors of the Parlor jingled as Mike ran inside.

"Guys! It's Nick, he— whoa, what is this?" he panted, nearly tripping over the glass panels and fish tank supplies scattered across the floor.

"New addition to the shop," Elli said, displaying her bagged fish. "What were you saying about Nick?"

"Oh, right," Mike recovered his train of thought. "He's coming, but he's not alone."

Sebastian regained his serious composure, watching the door. "What do you mean?"

The bells jingled again.

"I have some great news!" Nick announced, stepping inside. Indeed, he was not alone.

Arm-in-arm with Nick stood a beautiful woman. She was looking down bashfully, flowing dark hair falling over her shoulders, tastefully adorned by a white Valentino coat.

"And who is this?" Sebastian asked, already anticipating the answer.

Nick squeezed her gloved hand excitedly. "Boss, this is my wife! Angie, these are the others I work with: Sebastian, Elli, and, uh, Nolan."

"Noa," the redhead corrected quietly, studying the new person before him.

"Yeah, whatever," Nick went on. "Guys, this is Angelina."

The woman smiled, holding her hands together in a polite gesture. "Such a pleasure to meet you all." Her voice was melodic, carrying a thick Italian accent.

"Angelina," Elli repeated pensively, tilting her head to the side. "The Angelina that, if I recall correctly, screwed your only brother and ruined your life, Nicky? *That* Angelina?"

Nick coughed. "Uh, well." He looked away awkwardly as Angelina took a step forward.

"I know that I may never fully repent for my actions," she said. "I was careless, and I truly am sorry. I can only pray that my dear Nicolo can find it in his heart to forgive me. I thank you all for taking him in when he had no one."

"What made you decide to come find him after half a decade?" Sebastian asked.

Angelina stroked Nick's arm lovingly. "I have spent all this time searching for him! I left *La Cosa Nostra*. I could not bear to be without him."

"I see." Sebastian locked eyes with Nick. "A word outside please? Alone."

Nick, blushing faintly from Angelina's comment, nodded back and pried himself reluctantly from her embrace. He followed Sebastian outside, doors shutting behind them with a jingle.

Noa watched the drama unfold, furiously taking mental notes. He didn't know Nick had a wife, let alone an unfaithful one. And his superiors would be pleased with information about Niagara Co.'s connections to the Cosa Nostra, the infamous Sicilian mafia.

Angelina looked to Mike and Elli, ignoring Noa's presence. "Are you two friends of Nico?" She eyed Elli suspiciously. "Perhaps more that friends?"

Elli gagged. "Ew! No ma'am, he's all yours."

"He's our pal," Mike said. "He talks about you a lot. Especially when he's drunk."

"Does he?" Angelina smiled. "Good things, *si?*"

Mike ran a hand through his hair. "Uh. Sure."

She glanced at the door, behind which Sebastian and Nick were talking. "Is that handsome young man really your leader?"

"He's more than capable," Mike snapped.

Elli drummed her fingers on the counter. "What do you hope to accomplish here, anyway? Why come back to Nick? Why now?"

Angelina sighed, sitting at a pink table. "I want to start over, with him. I want to settle down, perhaps have children. I am not getting any younger and, well, I would rather be here with Nico than back home without him."

Elli laughed harshly. "Nick? A father? Good luck with that."

"Think what you must," Angelina said. "I understand your judgments. But I do love him still and want to spend the rest of my life with him."

"Wasn't it dangerous for you to come all the way here?" Mike asked.

"You underestimate how much I wished to find Nico," she replied, putting a hand to her chest. "Danger means nothing to me, not anymore."

Elli looked to Mike, then back to Angelina. "Well, I guess we don't really know your side of the story. Want some ice cream?"

Angelina smiled a beautiful smile. "I would love some, *cara mia*."

"Alright, Nick," Sebastian said as soon as the door shut behind them. "Start talking."

"Boss, I said some nasty things about Angie in the past, but I think she really changed!" Nick said. "She was so happy to see me. On the whole trip back, she kept apologizin' and saying she loved me. Can you believe she's still wearing her wedding band? I gotta find mine now too."

Sebastian raised an eyebrow. "After all that's happened, you trust her?"

Nick nodded. "And you can trust her too! It's the

biggest crime to betray the Cosa Nostra. If she left them to come here to me, she made a huge decision."

"No offense Nick, but why would she do that? You told me before that she was high up on the hierarchy. And direct lineage of the Luciano family?"

"Well, I guess she finally came to her senses," Nick boasted. "Love's a powerful thing, Boss. She's a changed woman, and she wants to be with me."

Sebastian had never seen Nick this happy before. He sighed. "Don't show her the underground. She can come to the Parlor and the Luna but stay with her at your place or get her a hotel room nearby."

"But Boss—"

"That's an order," he said sternly.

"Fine," Nick raised his hands. "But you're wrong about Angie."

"I hope I am. For your sake."

- Niagara Falls. Sunday, February 23, 2014 - 5:30 PM

Noa lay flat on his stomach on the floor of his living room, together with his laptop and a sprawling mess of papers and notes.

Whatever Elli had been planning for yesterday was pushed to this evening, and Noa was absolutely prohibited from entering the Polar Parlor until sundown.

They had wasted the majority of Saturday installing the new aquarium and filling it with a variety of tropical fish. The massive tank was at least four feet tall and sat on the western wall of the Parlor. Despite initial protests, Elli was ecstatic with the new addition to her shop and immediately adjusted the menu with a new flavor: Arctic Aqua.

Noa considered messaging Agent Koven to show off his

excellent bluffing abilities, but decided against it, considering their last conversation nearly removed him from the investigation. Nick's recently un-estranged wife Angelina helped out with the fish tank installation, giving Noa a chance to observe her interactions with the other members. When she had stepped out to use the ladies' room, Sebastian told them all to keep the underground a secret.

He was clearly on guard around this mysterious woman, but she was friendly and polite, and Nick endlessly assured them that she was trustworthy. Noa wondered if Sebastian would put her through a similar initiation test as his own.

He did a quick search of the CSIS database for Cosa Nostra crime families, following the lineages and coastal movements to find Nick and Angelina. He wasn't shocked to learn that Nick was from the Italian mob, although this one was much more prestigious than Noa could have imagined.

On a separate screen, he wrote up a short report to his boss about Nicolo "Nick" Benetti and minimized it, turning instead to the handwritten notes scattered around him.

Noa lit a cigarette and sat up. If the Niagara Co. had ties to California, then they likely had ties to other states as well, not just along the Great Lakes. This would make tracking down the whole group an extremely difficult task.

However, Noa reasoned, the insider trading was definitely taking place *here*. He already determined that Sebastian was the primary decision-maker – that much was clear. The only problem was figuring out how he got the information.

In messy handwriting, Noa consolidated the information he gathered on the Niagara Co. members on a note pad.

Niagara Company (New York state)

<u>Elli</u> (Elizabeth? Elise?) last name n/a

- mid-twenties
- blonde, green eyes, petite, from the South
- good at poker & cards
- runs ice cream shop (Polar Parlor)
- Niagara Co. accountant? broker? travels to Wall St. does she have financial background?
- past unknown

<u>Mike Levy</u>

- around thirty
- brown hair, brown eyes, not tall or short, average white guy
- right-hand man to Nové despite no apparent skills
- infatuated with Lucy (see below)
- past irrelevant; met Nové after suicide attempt

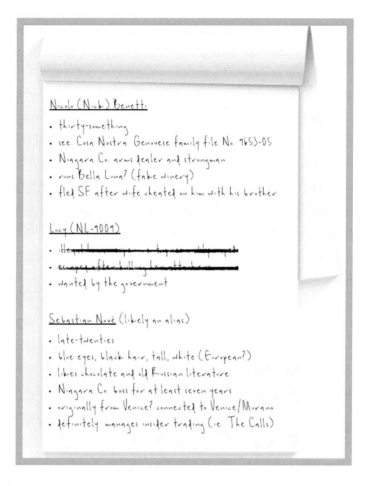

Nicolo (Nick) Benetti
- thirty-something
- see Cosa Nostra Genovese family file No. 7653-05
- Niagara Co. arms dealer and strongman
- runs Bella Luna? (fake winery)
- fled SF after wife cheated on him with his brother

Lucy (NL-7007)
- ~~Illegal~~
- ~~escaped after killing her attackers~~
- wanted by the government

Sebastian Nové (likely an alias)
- late-twenties
- blue eyes, black hair, tall, white (European?)
- likes chocolate and old Russian literature
- Niagara Co. boss for at least seven years
- originally from Venice? connected to Venice/Murano
- definitely manages insider trading (ie The Calls)

As he scribbled away, a knock sounded at the door.

Noa's pen froze on the paper. By this point, he knew only Elli and Sebastian had his address, and Elli was occupied with some activity at the Parlor.

"One sec!" Noa called as he quickly piled his notes on top of one another and shoved them under his bed. He kept his personal computer out but closed everything other than a music streaming program and Reddit.

He opened the door as calmly as possible. His reasoning was justified: Sebastian stood in the doorway, a look of irritation marring his features.

"Noa," he said without waiting for an invitation. "I need you to do something for me."

Noa stepped aside so he could enter. "What is it?"

"You've shown yourself to be talented with technology. I have a bad feeling about Nick's 'wife,'" Sebastian said as he walked inside and stopped in front of the open laptop. "Were you sitting on the floor? Do you need a desk?"

"No, no, it's fine!" Noa picked up the computer, placing it on the kitchen counter. "What do you need?"

"I can get you a desk," Sebastian said with genuine concern. "It pains me to see you living in such squalor."

"Please! Just tell me what's going on," Noa begged. "What happened?"

Sebastian sighed, leaning against the kitchen counter. "Nothing happened. I simply don't believe Angelina to be trustworthy. Is there a way you could access her phone records?"

Noa scratched an imaginary beard, pretending to consider the idea. "No," he lied, knowing that to do so, he would need to use government-issued software. "I don't think so. At least, not without her phone."

"Unfortunate," Sebastian said. "She never leaves it unsupervised. What about her email?"

"Probably," Noa paused again, for dramatic effect. "I could, if you know the email address."

Sebastian retrieved his cellphone from his coat pocket, sending a text. "Wonderful. Elli should have it. She demanded Angelina's family recipe for cannoli this morning." An immediate buzz displayed a reply from Elli, and he flipped the screen to Noa.

Barely 24 hours and he already suspects her, Noa thought with unease, pulling up the necessary online tools. "What, um, made you suspicious of Angelina? Did she do anything strange?"

"Not particularly," Sebastian replied. "Call it a hunch."

"Just a gut feeling?" Noa asked, typing in the email and running a password cracker.

"They say a hunch is your brain's shortcut to the truth," Sebastian said. "But some of her actions do warrant suspicion. When Nick offered her a hotel room, she demanded to stay with him instead. And she wants to follow him everywhere."

"What if she just wants to be with him?" Noa offered.

"Perhaps. Or she wants to know the location of his home. Also, it strikes me as odd that she would abandon her position in La Cosa Nostra to be with Nick."

"With all due respect sir," Noa half-smiled, "haven't you ever been in love?"

Sebastian shot him a look. "Excuse me?"

"Never mind," Noa flushed, focusing on the monitor. "Okay! I'm in her inbox."

"That was quick," Sebastian said, peering at the screen. "Have you done this before?"

"Um, no, but I read a lot about it." Noa kicked himself for getting into the account so quickly. He needed to change the subject. "Look, there's a recent email with an attachment from the police."

"Open it."

> **Deputy Chief D. Perea**
> Plea Bargain Agreement [Conditional]
> To: Angelina Benetti
>
> 📥 Inbox
>
> Angelina Benetti-Luciano,
>
> Attached is a copy of the contract which you have signed on **[December 13, 2013]** with the San Francisco Police Department and the District Attorney of Napa County High Courts outlining your conditional plea agreement.
>
> As per the agreement, for a reduced sentence of **[5 years - time served]**, you must:
>
> - Locate and establish contact with **[Nicolo Benetti]** (hereafter "the target")
> - Determine the target's base of operations and current status
> - Report target's whereabouts to **Deputy Chief of Special Operations [John Sanford]**
>
> Failure to do the above will result in termination of plea agreement.
>
> Contact me or your attorney if you have any questions.
>
> **Daniel Perea | Deputy Chief of Operations**
> San Francisco Police Department, Napa County
> 1251 3rd St, San Francisco, CA | 94158 USA
>
> 📄 SFPD_Plea_Agr
> mnt_A_...ti.docx

Sebastian made a *tsk* sound. "Disappointing, but not surprising."

"Holy shit," Noa stared at the screen. "She's working for the cops?"

Sebastian ignored the question, going to the door. "Thank you, Noa. That will do."

"Wait, what will you do now?" Noa closed the laptop anxiously. "What about this deputy chief guy? Doesn't this mean they already know your location? And what about Nick?"

"Come with me if you want to know," Sebastian replied, just above a whisper. "It's time we invite our friend Angelina for tea."

The drive across the border to the Queen of Spades café was eerily quiet. Noa kept his attention on the Niagara River, raging on beyond his window, his hands subconsciously gripping his laptop tightly.

At the entrance to the tearoom, Sebastian asked Maria for the Queen's special. Without the need for any further elaboration, Maria escorted the two of them through a locked back door, down a set of stairs and through a long hallway.

Every fiber of Noa's being screamed to run away. The air was cold and smelled faintly of iron and salt. The floor seemed uneven and the ceiling hung lower than normal. At the end of the narrow hall stood a metal door which led them into a spacious chamber, resembling an interrogation room with a separate viewing area.

The viewing section, which had a couple of chairs and an intercom on a small table, faced a window into the empty interrogation room.

Maria gestured to the chairs. "You need water? Tea?"

"No thank you, Maria," Sebastian said politely, sitting down. "We shouldn't be here long."

"Okay. Wait here," she said as she departed, locking the door behind her.

Noa stood by the wall, laptop pressed to his chest. "Um. So, what now?"

Sebastian turned to Noa, as if just now remembering his presence. "We await our guest," he said bluntly. "Have a seat."

Hesitantly, Noa sat in the chair nearby. He tensed when the door opened again to Maria's return.

"They are here," she said.

"Thank you, Maria." Sebastian stood, offering his seat to her. "Could you lend me your laptop, Noa?"

"Oh, sure," Noa passed it over, ensuring the screen would unlock to Angelina's traitorous email. As he did so, Maria sat beside him without a word.

Laptop in hand, Sebastian left the room. In a few moments, Noa saw him appear on the other side of the window, placing his computer on the desk inside. Shortly after, two more figures entered the interrogation room. Lucy and Angelina.

Noa shifted in his seat. "Can they see us?" he asked Maria.

"No. Cannot hear us either," she replied in her thick Eastern European accent.

Sebastian waited until Angelina sat down before doing the same, facing her across the table. Lucy stood off to the side, examining her nails.

Angelina took in her surroundings, eyes darkening. "*Dove siamo?*"

"*Per favore, parli in inglese,*" Sebastian said. "I just want to talk, Angelina."

She scowled at the mirror, facing him again. "*Vaffanculo, bastardo. Tè del pomeriggio,* hm?"

While Noa had some knowledge of Italian, he didn't know what she said – but enough to know that it was colorful.

Barely glancing up from her manicure, Lucy seized Angelina by the hair and pulled, forcing her to meet Lucy's blank stare from behind her seat. "English," she said.

Angelina grit her teeth, grabbing Lucy by the wrist. "You forget where I come from, *puttana*. You'll regret leaving my hands untied." She rose to her feet, swinging a punch at Lucy's face.

Her fist grazed Lucy's cheek. She carefully smoothed down her scarf to the back of her shirt and wiped a small speck of blood from her mouth, subsequently returning the assault with a kick to Angelina's stomach.

The two women attacked one another, a flurry of black and pink swirling in the room. Noa watched in horror, gripping the edges of his chair.

Maria chuckled beside him. "Do not worry. Lucy is just humoring your guest. A tired suspect speaks more willingly."

In a few short moments, a scream sliced through the room and Noa heard a petrifying crack. Lucy had pinned Angelina onto the table, headfirst, and was holding her arm behind her back.

Angelina squirmed beneath her weight, crying out. "*Basta, basta!*"

"That's enough, Luce," Sebastian said. Lucy stepped aside, leaving Angelina to cradle her broken arm with the other. "Can we speak now, *signora*?"

Angelina exhaled a shaky breath. "What do you want from me?

"Tell me why you're here," Sebastian said.

"To be with Nico, of course!" she spat. "Why else?"

From the corner of the interrogation room, Lucy scoffed under her breath.

Sebastian leaned forward in his chair. "We both know that's not true."

"With god as my witness, I tell you this is the truth," Angelina said.

"No need to bring god into this," he said. "See, I'm just a little confused. What would you, Angelina Luciano of the legendary Cosa Nostra, be doing way out here? Surely it isn't because you love Nick, no, because then you wouldn't have fucked his brother and stood idly by when Nick murdered his only sibling. Don't you agree, Luce?"

Noa marveled at the calmness in Sebastian's voice, barely grasping the newest revelation about Nick's past. He watched as Lucy nodded her head emphatically.

"That begs the question, then," Sebastian continued, "what would make you change your mind after all these years? Last chance to tell me."

Angelina's lips curled into a slim smirk. "Mistakes happen. Why should I tell you anything? I am pure blood Cosa Nostra. You speak the tongue, but I can see you are no Italiano. Your accent is Venetian, but you use mainland slang. And your features," she sneered. "I don't recognize. What are you really? German? Polish?"

"Pure blood Cosa Nostra? I suppose that makes sense," Sebastian said, opening Noa's laptop. "Which one started working with the feds first, Valachi? Or Cafaro? A nice legacy."

Angelina said nothing, staring at the email on the screen.

"Last question, and I suggest you reply honestly." Sebastian closed the computer. "What *exactly* did you tell the SFPD?"

Her voice shook with anger. "I tell you nothing."

"Is that your final answer?" Sebastian asked, with some exasperation.

Angelina spat. "*Sei sordo* e *stupido*?"

Simultaneously, Lucy and Sebastian glanced in the mirror.

Before he could protest, Maria had moved behind Noa's chair and covered his eyes with her hands. After which, the sound of screaming overtook his senses.

Shaken to the core and unable to move, Noa struggled to breathe evenly. He could feel the color draining from his face.

Finally, he heard Angelina's desperate plea: "Stop! *Vi prego, per favore!*"

Then Sebastian's voice, asking: "What did you tell them?"

"Everything," she cried out. "I don't care what happens to that scum."

Maria removed her hands, and as the fog cleared from Noa's glasses he couldn't hold back the gasp that escaped him. Smears of blood stained the floor and table, and he could see that Angelina's fingers were wrangled into impossible positions. Her nose was broken, and a few teeth lay to side of Lucy's right foot.

He covered his mouth in an attempt contain the fear and vomit threatening to break free. Lucy had retreated to the back of the interrogation room, inspecting the hem of her scarf for damage.

"I already told them," Angelina said hoarsely with some satisfaction. "The police will be coming to your shithole town to arrest Nicolo and take him where he belongs. To wither away in jail with the rest of his family."

With a disappointed sigh, Sebastian glanced to the microphone on the table. "Catch that, Nick?"

From elsewhere in the building, Nick's weary voice traveled through the intercom. "Loud and clear, Boss."

Angelina broke into a sharp laugh. "Oh, you're watching too, are you, *te stronzo?*" She glowered at the microphone. "Coward! You dare let a *woman* beat me half to death – you can't even do it yourself! I never loved you. Rot in hell, Nicolo."

Before she could speak more, Lucy brought down both fists over her head, knocking her out. Noa looked away, teetering on the edge of the chair.

"Sorry you had to hear that, Nick." Sebastian stood

from the interrogation room table. "Maria, I'll be in touch later regarding our friend. For now, we need to deal with the police situation."

He and Lucy left Angelina's motionless body in the interrogation room.

"E-excuse me," Noa's voice cracked as he stood slowly. He bolted to the corner trash can, expelling the contents of his lunch.

Maria stepped aside when Sebastian re-entered the viewing area.

"...Perhaps it was a bit soon to bring him with me," Sebastian said apologetically.

"You think?" Maria shook her head, leaving them alone.

Sebastian put a hand on Noa's head softly. "Sorry you had to see that. I did not expect this must resistance from her."

Trembling, Noa clutched the bin with shaky hands. *This is what they do to traitors,* he thought in horror. *This is what they'd do to me.*

Sebastian crouched beside him, rubbing his back. "Hey, come on. No need to be afraid. Lucy could have done much worse if she wanted to."

Noa shuddered, hurling into the trash can again.

"Right, maybe not the time to point that out," Sebastian muttered. "Apologies, I'm not the best at judging others' tolerance. No more missions or interrogations, alright? No shame in that."

Noa's thoughts swirled in a panicked haze. *I have to get out. I have to finish my investigation and get the hell out before they kill me.*

"Can you walk?" Sebastian helped the boy up, keeping an arm under him for support.

Noa managed a slight nod and the two of them joined Lucy in the narrow hall.

"I'll take you home, but we'll swing by the Parlor. Elli's orders," Sebastian said. "And you should probably change, Lucy."

Lucy looked down at her clothes, which were crusting with blood. She shrugged in agreement and followed them out through a hidden exit.

It took the entirety of Noa's concentration to keep the bile down during their drive back across the border. Angelina's screams played on loop in his mind, echoing like a broken record.

"Noa, if you're not feeling well, I can just take you back," Sebastian offered as they pulled up to the Polar Parlor. "But decide fast, because I need to return to handle Nick's affairs."

"It's okay," Noa croaked, practically leaping out of the car and inhaling the cold March air. "I just need some water."

"Alright, no problem." Sebastian opened the Parlor's doors, ushering Noa inside.

SEVEN
MOTIVATION

The moment Noa stepped foot in the shop, Elli and Mike jumped out from behind the counter, popping streamers and confetti guns into the air.

A banner hung along the back wall that read *Welcome to the team, Noa!* and balloons floated among the snowflakes near the ceiling.

Already on edge and caught off guard by the sudden noise, Noa passed out in an instant.

"Oh dear." Sebastian caught him before he hit the floor. "Perhaps not the right time."

Elli's mouth fell open. "What? What happened? Where were you guys? I've been planning this for days! Where are Nick and Angie?"

Sebastian groaned. "This is a small team. Our communication could stand to be improved." He picked up the teenager, draping him over his shoulder. "Forget all that. Clean this up immediately; we have some uninvited guests on the way."

Noa awoke on a familiar couch.

He sat up, adjusting his glasses. He was alone in Sebastian's subterranean office. He checked his phone to see how much time had passed and realized it was already late evening.

Why was he alone? Noa stood, dubiously approaching Sebastian's desk. They were probably dealing with the SFPD or whomever Angelina contacted about Nick's location. Depending on the convincing required, Noa would have the office to himself for a while.

With every blink, he saw the scene from the interrogation room. Noa shoved his hair back away from his face. He had to finish the job and get out.

Swallowing his fear, he began investigating the office. The adrenaline from the day's events spurred him on. That, and the knowledge that he couldn't afford to be here any longer.

Noa sifted through the desk drawers. Most of them were locked, but the ones that opened had a first aid kit, some folders, chocolates and a few books. Noa leafed through the folders but found no relevant information.

The chocolates caught his eye, though. He took one out, examining it in the light. A European brand that seemed familiar. *Did Sebastian import them?*

He slammed the drawer shut, looking around. A post-it on the desk-top phone had three stock tickers written in pen. Noa furrowed his brows in frustration, knowing he must be close.

Something in this room, he thought. *Something hidden from sight. You wouldn't hide anything important in a drawer – anyone could pry those open.*

Noa searched the floor under the desk and under the couch. Unsuccessful, he moved on to the wall. He ran a hand along the plaster, a little higher than was comfortable, to mimic Sebastian's height.

There it was. Noa felt a shift under his fingers as a number pad revealed itself on the wall.

He gasped quietly, examining the buttons. He touched his hand to the same spot and the lock hid itself again. Noa bit his lip excitedly.

But what about the code? Sebastian wore gloves most of the time, so fingerprints wouldn't help. Noa also didn't know how many digits it required. He was certain that whatever sat inside the locked wall compartment held the answer to the insider information. He could practically *taste* it; he was so close! If he could just try enough times, surely, he would figure it out—

The handle of the office door clicked open.

Noa stumbled back over to the couch quickly, grateful to all that is holy that he re-hid the number pad.

Sebastian entered the office, holding a takeout bag and a steaming mug. "Hey, there. Feeling any better? I brought you some tea and food."

Noa nodded. "Thank you, but I'm not really that hungry."

"I figured as much. At least have some tea." Sebastian placed the bag on his desk, handing him the cup.

Noa held in his hands but didn't drink, staring at the liquid instead to avoid looking at the wall where the safe was hidden. "Thanks. Did the cops come?"

"Yes, just two detectives. Luckily, they were already suspicious of Angelina, so they didn't cause us too much trouble. They believe she blew them off and ran. They'll spend their time and effort trying to find her," he said.

Noa cleared his throat. "And, um. Will they ever find her?"

Sebastian sat down on the couch beside him. "Noa, listen. This is a dangerous line of business. Sometimes I have to make unfortunate choices to protect my team. I understand if this frightened you," he glanced at Noa, "and if you want to leave."

Noa's eyes went wide. *Leave? He's offering me a way out?*

This was a chance to escape the Niagara Co. alive and never look back. He'd have other cases, right? His boss would understand.

But the *safe*! It was *so close*. And he already spent so much time on this case.

Noa shook his head in earnest. "No! I don't want to leave. I just– I wasn't expecting that. But I'm part of the team, aren't I?"

With a look of what seemed like relief, Sebastian smiled. "Of course, you are. I'm glad you want to stay. What's keeping you here, despite the constant dangers?"

"Lots!" Noa exclaimed, nearly spilling the tea. "I feel like I owe it to everyone after that mission where I thought you died. And I like spending time with Elli and Mike in the ice cream shop. And you got me those fish..." his voice trailed off.

"Noa? What's wrong?" Sebastian asked, taking the mug from him worriedly and placing it on the desk.

Noa slowly came to the realization that he wasn't lying about any of those reasons. But he was likewise petrified by the prospect of being found out.

He lowered his gaze, clasping his hands together. "I-I'm just a little shaken up."

Sebastian nodded, standing up. "Of course. You need some rest and it's getting late now, so how about I take you home?"

But the safe! I need a chance to crack it!

Noa hesitated. "Wait!" Without realizing it, he grabbed Sebastian's wrist. "Can I stay here for the night?"

Sebastian studied his face. "You want to stay here? In my office?"

"Can I?" Noa pleaded. "I don't want to be alone. Can I stay with you?"

An unfamiliar expression flickered over Sebastian's face. "Noa. I think I know what you're doing."

Noa froze, feeling the walls shift closer. "I don't know what you mean."

"I think you do," Sebastian said.

The air stalled in Noa's lungs as he imagined the horrible things that awaited him at Lucy's hands. Before he could muster a reply, Sebastian leaned down over him, mere inches from his face.

"Are you trying to seduce me?"

Noa, caught in the deep grasp of those piercing blue eyes, floundered for a response. "I... I..." A marginally better outcome than he expected, but he couldn't say yes. And yet, if he said no? The only other conclusion would be that he was spying. "I..."

"You really have an astounding number of freckles. Like constellations." Sebastian placed a hand to Noa's cheek gingerly. "But don't go that route. Trust me."

At a loss for words, Noa felt himself flushing. Definitely not how he expected his investigation to turn out.

Sebastian stood again, smoothing down his jacket. "Come on. I'll take you home."

EIGHT

RETURN

- Niagara Falls. Wednesday, February 26, 2014

"Alrighty, for the ladies, we've got a Caramel Macchiato for Lucy and an Americano for Elli," Mike listed off as he handed out the morning's beverages, "a regular Mocha for the Boss, and a plain cup of black for me, and uh. Oh."

Mike stopped and held the empty coffee tray awkwardly once he placed his own drink down at his spot. "Nick, buddy! Didn't think you'd make it to the team meeting today."

Entering the 6th-below-ground conference room, Nick took his usual seat. Solemn and weary, an imaginary cloud loomed over his head, casting deeper shadows on his face than usual.

"Yeah, don't worry about the coffee," he said in a hoarse voice. "I just wanted to take my mind off things."

Elli rested her chin atop a folded Polar Parlor apron, watching Nick from her periphery. "I believe what Mike is *trying* to say is we're a bit surprised to see you here after all that's happened. Thanks for filling me in by the way, Luce."

Lucy nodded, sipping her macchiato.

"I swear, I had no idea Angie was a *pentito*," Nick said. "Why would I be here for five years? And be here still? She's fuckin' played me too!"

"Maybe you should take a day to rest though?" Mike offered. "The new kid's got the day off too!"

"Nah, I'm good, really." Nick rubbed at his temples. "Chief? What's your call?"

At the head of the conference room table, Sebastian was scrolling through his phone, very slightly spinning side-to-side in the revolving chair.

"These offices would be nicer with windows," he said pensively, without looking up from the device. "What do you think of Palmer Ave. and Simcoe?"

Apart from the sound of the swivel chair and Lucy drinking her coffee, the room was quiet.

Eventually, he lowered the phone. "Sorry, did I miss something?"

"Are you all there this morning, Bassie?" Elli tapped at her forehead. "Maybe *you* need a day off?"

"Boss, weren't you the one that wanted the underground in the first place?" Mike asked. "What's this all about?"

Sebastian put his cell away, folding his hands together. "Well, thanks to our guest from the West, there is a chance that this location may be compromised. We may need to seal the underground access from the Parlor and winery soon, until we have a back-up plan – use the Falls entrances in the meantime to access the vault."

"Sure, that all makes sense," Elli said, "but what's this about windows? And what does this mean for the Parlor and Bella Luna?"

Sebastian shrugged. "Natural sunlight would be nice,

don't you agree? The second-floor office above the Parlor, for example, but it's too cramped for anything other than status updates. As for the businesses themselves, they should operate as usual for now."

Elli raised a brow. "Right. Back to the topic of Nicky's screw up, do we think this is a standalone incident? Or related to our dead horse in Washington?"

"It's standalone," Nick grumbled. "I looked into it. Plea deals for Cosa Nostra squealers."

Mike pat him on the back. "That's rough, buddy."

"We'll need another connection in the West," Sebastian said. "Until Washington is in the clear."

Nick sighed. "I'll see what I can do."

"Markets open in thirty," Elli said, flipping open a notebook she pulled out from under the apron in front of her. "I earmarked the trades you sent me this morning, Bassie. Should I make the call on those for today?"

"Yes, just those three," Sebastian confirmed, picking up his phone again.

Elli hesitated. "There were four. Three stocks, plus gold on the Comex."

"Hm? Oh, yes," he nodded. "Whatever I sent you earlier. By the way, where is Noa?"

Mike chuckled. "You're really out of it today, Boss. Elli gave him the day off, remember?"

"I hope he'll actually get some sleep and rest up," she said. "Instead of playing that stupid Tetris game all day."

Sebastian stood suddenly, his chair impacting the wall behind him with a bang.

"Boss? What's wrong?" Mike asked.

"I need to go," he said, making his way to the door. "Business trip. I'll be back tomorrow."

"Huh? You're leaving now?" Elli sat up. "Where?"

"You're in charge, Elli," he said in response, halfway out of the room. "Mike, I'll send you some potential properties to look into. Ciao."

Elli watched him leave. "What is up with him today? He never mentioned any trip."

"Seems distracted," Lucy murmured, tossing an empty coffee cup into the trash.

"You're right about that, Luce," Elli said. "What was with that look?"

- Monaco. Thursday, February 27, 2014 -

A chilled, marine breeze off the cliffs of Monte Carlo beckoned with it the whisper of spring in the French Riviera.

As the regional train pulled away from the station, Sebastian felt overcome with melancholy and a profound sense of loneliness.

For the first time in eleven years, he retraced familiar routes around the small Mediterranean coastline. The arching alleyways. The brilliantly blue marinas. The towering palm trees, lining pristine city streets and cobblestone paths.

He stopped, unintentionally, at the entrance to an old pier in Fontvielle. Drawn to the water's edge, Sebastian knew the reason for the growing pit of sorrow swirling at the edges of his memory. The absence and the longing.

Lucciana's lighthouse was gone. All 70 of its rusty steps, and crumbling brick walls, and splintered wooden crates — perfect for catching the sunrise. Perfect for watching the waves. Perfect for middle-of-the-night conversation about the future. Gone.

Broken from his reverie by a passing gull, Sebastian resumed his mission.

He soon stood before the looming gates of St. Isidore, just as vile and oppressive as he recalled them. He couldn't bring himself to ring the bell. The domineering presence of the building made him feel like a child again – naive and manipulated and at their mercy.

An involuntary shiver travelled down his spine as he regretted the choice to come here in person. There must have been another way to make contact. Anything would be better than returning to this wretched place.

"Ça va, monsieur?"

Sebastian snapped back to reality. Two teen girls in matching grey uniforms eyed him questioningly through the gate.

He kneeled down, meeting their height. "Good morning. Is there a November currently attending this institution?"

The girls looked to each other for a moment.

"Yes," said the slightly older of the two. "Do you know him?"

Sebastian nodded. "Maybe. Does he have bright red hair? Freckles?"

The younger girl spoke up. "Oh, you mean the 15th Gen. November. No, he's gone. He left a while ago."

That involuntary shiver returned. "What do you mean, he 'left?' Did he graduate? Or?"

"I don't know," the older girl said with a disinterested shrug. "We weren't close."

"None of us really knew him," the younger one added. "One day we just noticed he wasn't here anymore."

"I see," Sebastian said. "Do you remember anything about him? His specialties? Any physical characteristics? Did he wear glasses?"

The girls tensed up, glancing over their shoulders as a tall figure approached behind them.

"March, August. That would be enough."

"Yes, Sister!" The girls chirped in unison, darting towards the inner courtyard.

Sebastian straightened up, meeting the cold stare of his old headmistress through the iron bars.

"Sister Ingrid," he said. "St. Isidore does not allow for a retirement package?"

She studied him dubiously. "Do I know you, *monsieur?*"

Sebastian pretended to clutch his chest in a dramatic gesture. "You wound me, Sister. Do you treat all your 'prodigies' this way, or just the ones that don't work out?"

Sister Ingrid's eyes widened in realization. "Our runaway September?"

"I need to speak to Emilio," he said.

"Always a thorn in my side, despite all of your supposed 'potential,'" she said disparagingly. "Your little disappearing act cost us greatly."

Sebastian withheld a scoff. "It warms my heart to hear that, truly."

"We had multiple bidders lined up for your graduation," the sister said, sliding into a lecturing tone. "Prestigious positions, each and every one. Father Emilio had to personally handle the reputational damage done as a result of your egregious actions."

"Do you expect me to apologize?" Sebastian's gloved hands curled into fists inside his coat pockets. "After what you did to Seb— November? And then concocted some convoluted lie about a bee sting."

"Ah. Yes, that poor boy," Sister Ingrid crossed herself. "It was a calculated risk."

Sebastian slammed the iron gates. A few kids in the garden turned to face their direction.

"You disgust me," he growled. "You and this entire establishment."

"Sister Ingrid. Surely this is not the best place for a discussion. Shall we let our guest through?"

Sebastian knew the owner of that voice. With the two young girls from earlier at his sides, St. Isidore's headmaster rested a hand on Sister Ingrid's shoulder, his other leaning on a wooden walking stick.

"If you insist, Father." The Sister unlocked the front gates, reluctantly allowing Sebastian through.

March and August peered up at him curiously, before the headmistress shooed them away.

"Come, let us continue in my office," Father Emilio said, already making his way toward the courtyard.

A mixture of rage, fear and regret whirled around in Sebastian's mind, giving way to overwhelming emptiness upon entering the grounds of St. Isidore. He stayed quiet as they passed by the gardens, adorned by soon-to-blossom flowers and soon-to-pollinate bees, and the statue of their Patron Saint, and into the halls of the building proper.

"Welcome home, September," Father Emilio said once they were out of the cold. "I hardly recognized you without that long yellow hair."

Sebastian tensed. "I won't be staying."

"No, I figured not," Emilio nodded, slowly walking towards the ornate doors at the end of the hall.

Sebastian kept his hands in his pockets and his head down, unable or unwilling to take in the surroundings. The claustrophobic classrooms. The winding staircase to the children's rooms upstairs. The bolted entrance to the downstairs—

"September, wait up!"

Instinctively, Sebastian spun around.

A teenage girl with dark brown pigtails wearing a St. Isidore uniform rushed by him, running into the library. A younger boy chased after her, carrying a stack of heavy books.

Father Emilio stopped at his office, hand on the handle. "Your successor. The 15th September. Gifted in chemistry and physics – she will be graduating soon."

Sebastian said nothing, watching them disappear into the library.

"Shall we?" Father Emilio opened the door, stepping inside and taking a seat behind his desk.

Unchanged by time, the headmaster's office was just as Sebastian pictured it in his most unwanted memories. He closed the door and sat down.

"So, how can I help you, September?" Father Emilio leaned his walking stick against the drawers and put on a pair of thin rimmed glasses. "My, you really have grown."

"Tell me about November," Sebastian said in an even tone.

"Which one? There have been many."

Sebastian narrowed his eyes. "The 15th."

"Ah. Yes." The headmaster clasped his hands in front of him atop the desk. "A bright boy. Your departure affected him greatly. But, as we say, *perfer et obdura*..."

An icy chill enveloped the room. "Where is he now?"

"I cannot disclose that information," Father Emilio said firmly.

Sebastian grit his teeth. "You can't or you won't? Did he graduate? Or leave on his own? To what did he change his name?"

"Information about St. Isidore students, past or present,

is strictly confidential," the headmaster reiterated. "I would not even share anything about you, September, if anyone came to ask."

"Fine. At least tell me this: did anything change about him physically? Since I left?"

Emilio sighed. "Physically? His eyesight did worsen over the years from prolonged staring at computer screens, so we had to get him glasses when he was around ten or so. And I suppose this is not a physical trait but as a teenager he picked up Sister Mary's vice when he found her smoking in the cemetery."

The chill intensified as jagged pieces of a jigsaw puzzle clicked into place.

"I see," Sebastian said quietly, standing from the chair.

Father Emilio watched him intently. "You know, September, we truly had our work cut out for us when you decided to run. Such a selfish, immature decision. I had expected better of you."

Opting to face the door instead of the speaker, Sebastian exhaled a sharp breath. "Right. Because I failed to live up to my 'high potential' and tarnished the school's fine reputation."

"Yes, that was a problem." Emilio agreed. "However, it took us just as many months to fix the damage that your departure inflicted upon poor November."

"*Fix* the damage?" Sebastian echoed, suddenly struck by an onset of light-headedness. "What did you tell him? What did you do?"

Father Emilio tapped a finger against the oak desk. "November got it into his mind that you ran away because you learned the truth about him. About his past."

"What are you talking about?" Sebastian turned to face

him again. "You *know* exactly why I left. I don't know anything about November's life before Isidore!"

The headmaster shrugged. "Anything cracked will shatter at a touch. We worked with what we had."

Sebastian shook his head in disbelief. "So, you let him believe that I—"

"Yes," Emilio confirmed with an indifferent expression. "That you left because of him."

NINE
ST. ISIDORE – PART VII. ABANDONMENT

- Monaco. Winter, 2003 -

November obediently waited in the library for hours, reading and re-reading the same textbook. He would glance to the window once in a while, wondering with a slight pang of worry why September would spend so much time talking with July.

Is it true? he recalled her asking, as if accusing September of some wrongdoing.

He couldn't imagine September being in the wrong. His closest friend; his protector. Since his arrival in Monaco over a year ago, November hadn't left the blond's side. September seemed to hold a great deal of influence with the St. Isidore staff – because of his grades, November figured? – and shielded the boy from punishment whenever he could.

The Sisters were keen on punishment.

Head down, November kept his thoughts focused on the textbook's words, imaging them as colored blocks stacking atop one another.

"You're still here?"

He looked up. *July.*

"Where's September?" he asked, trying his best to sound calm.

She twirled the end of her long black braid on the tip of her finger. "You haven't heard?"

November swallowed uneasily. "Heard what?"

"He's gone."

Standing from the library table, November approached her slowly. "What... what do you mean?"

"Not that I particularly care," July sighed theatrically, towering over the redhead. "But it would appear he learned some unfortunate truth. And ran."

Unfortunate truth.

November's face drained of color. Pushing past July, he raced out of the library and up the spiralling staircase to the second floor, stopping at the entrance to his room. September's bedside drawers were cleared. Even his treasured rosary was missing.

Unable to comprehend the sight before him, November sped down to Father Emilio's office. *This simply could not be happening.*

September would not leave him like this. Months of late-night stories, hidden Belgian chocolates, stolen minutes on stolen video game consoles flashed before his eyes. *Misha* would not leave him like this.

He stopped before the thick oak door at the end of the hall and knocked frantically.

"Come in."

The boy pushed the door open with a shaky hand and stepped inside.

"Ah, November," Father Emilio said, peering over a file. "I've been meaning to speak with you."

"...Um." November's mouth was dry. "Where is September?"

Father Emilio placed his documents down. "September. Yes, where indeed?"

November clenched his fists, raising his voice. "Where *is* he?"

"How shall I put this?" The Headmaster removed his glasses, rubbing at the bridge of his nose. "September is no longer with us."

"No longer with..." November's voice faded away. His lip quivered. "What? He's dead?!"

Father Emilio did not respond.

"No, but... July said he ran. That he learned an unfortunate truth—" November's breathing quickened as cut himself off.

Unfortunate truth.

"Oh, November," Father Emilio said apologetically, standing from the desk. "This is for the best. You should never allow yourself to get too attached."

- Niagara Falls. Thursday, February 27, 2014 -

Noa awoke from a restless sleep to the sound of his ringtone.

In a groggy haze, he felt around his bedside for the cellphone and answered it, mumbling out a half-audible 'hello?'

"Are you still in bed?!" Elli shouted through the speaker, resulting in a wince from the teen. "You were supposed to be here half an hour ago!"

Noa squinted at the phone's clock for a few seconds, unable to make out the time. "I was? I-I mean, yeah! Sorry, I just, um. I wasn't feeling well."

He heard a sigh from the other end. "I know you had a rough weekend, hon'," Elli said softly. "And I'm sorry your welcome party didn't work out. But you've been off for days and I've got that UNICEF fundraiser with the Wall Streeters today and *you're supposed to help me.*"

"Right, of course," he said, sitting up slowly and searching around the bed for his glasses. "I'll be there as soon as I can!"

"Jeez, first Bassie, now you," she grumbled. "What's with everyone recently?"

Before Noa could inquire further, she hung up.

He let the phone drop into his lap and yawned. Truthfully, he had forgotten about the fundraiser entirely, and didn't even realize how many days came and went. He spent the majority of his time off in bed, engrossed in video games or napping, in an attempt to block out the existential dread of his current situation.

It was only mildly successful.

With his short vacation at an end, Noa begrudgingly got up and dressed for the day ahead. Before setting out to the Parlor, he sent his collection of compiled notes on the Niagara Co. to Agent Koven (careful to exclude any classified information on NL-9000), to maintain the image of a hardworking undercover agent. On the job, seven days a week.

Opting to substitute an actual breakfast that would take time to prepare for a cigarette, Noa was out the door less than fifteen minutes after Elli's call.

"Finally!" she exclaimed when he walked in through the Parlor's doors. "Okay – I've got Mike on catering and Nick is surprisingly not awful at decorations—"

"I heard that," Nick said.

"Anyway," she continued, "Bassie was supposed to take care of the entertainment but he's AWOL so that's fallen to me. Do you think you could stay here and just monitor the tickets and guests and whatnot?"

Noa blinked a few times, mesmerized at yet another one of the Polar Parlor's transformations. Now it resembled a venue fitting of a corporate party, complete with appetizer stations and lanyard name-tag tables and a painting of the Falls up for auction.

"Um, sure," he said finally. "Where did you say Sebastian went?"

"Darned if I know!" Elli threw her arms up dramatically. "Emergency business trip, was all he said yesterday."

"Huh." Noa thought that was strange. From the dynamics of this team, normally Mike at the very least would go with him.

"Okay, so you're all good here? Great! I need to go confirm the musicians," she said, running off into the back.

Noa nodded hesitantly, not entirely sure of his duties but hoping he'd figure it out eventually. He went behind the counter out of habit and absentmindedly nicked a cookie from the display.

His thoughts drifted to the events of Sunday night, unwillingly, and he shivered uncomfortably at the memory. The email, the interrogation, the safe. The convenient misunderstanding that may have saved his life. The drive back to his apartment in awkward silence as Queen's ill-fitting *Under Pressure* played on Sebastian's car radio.

And now the song was stuck in his head.

Suddenly uneasy, Noa made an attempt to shake the voices of Freddie Mercury and David Bowie out of his mind and focus instead on some fundraiser-related task. Once the event was over, he'd find some way to sneak into Sebastian's office and take another crack at the safe. Since he was away on business, it was the perfect opportunity.

By the afternoon, the fundraiser was in full swing. A classy jazz band played in the back of the Parlor and white-aproned waiters distributed sparkling drinks to mingling groups of people.

Elli had returned and repositioned Noa at the welcome station, despite his requests to avoid interacting with any of the guests. He handed out name-tags and Polar Parlor goodie bags with a robotic politeness to suit after suit, preoccupied with the ways he might try to break into the hidden office safe.

"My name won't be on your guest-list, I'm afraid." A familiar voice tore him out of his mental planning.

Startled out of his thoughts, Noa realized he was gripping the clipboard much too tightly. "Oh, hi! Hello," he stuttered. "You're back. I mean, Elli told me you went on a business trip. And now you're back. How was it?"

Sebastian seemed a bit distraught, dark circles around his eyes betraying a recent lack of any real rest. He glanced around the Parlor, crowded and almost at capacity. "Do you want to get out of here?" He said, ignoring Noa's question. "Go for a walk?"

"Yes!" Any despair at the undoing of his plans to try the safe again was overtaken by the relief at this offer. Noa nearly leaped over the desk before hesitating. "Oh, but Elli..."

"I'll tell her," Sebastian said. "They're just name-tags. I'm sure people will figure it out. Come on," he urged, pushing through a small crowd of people and out the door.

Noa followed, grateful to escape the congestion within the Parlor and inhale the outside air. It was one of the warmer days that late February had seen so far, but still cool and crisp, with a lingering winter wind blowing through the streets.

"Where are we going?" Noa asked after a few minutes of walking.

"Nowhere in particular," Sebastian replied. "I just felt like a walk. Have you been to the Falls yet?"

"No, actually," Noa thought back. "Well, technically, I guess we drove over them, and I've been under them."

Sebastian chuckled. "Doesn't count."

They walked a bit further, off the sidewalks of Old Falls St. and closer towards the river, until the quiet stillness between them was replaced by the roaring of the cascade.

Unable to contain a gasp, Noa ran ahead, marvelling at the sight.

As the sun pierced through the clouds, it turned the coursing waters of the river into a brilliant, emerald shade of green, lined with foamy bubbles at the jagged edges of its shores. Three colossal waterfalls, like legendary whirlpools, boomed with a hypnotizing rush.

Closest to their shore, the terrifying beauty of the Hell's Half Acre surging out into the American Falls was the most amazing sight he had ever seen.

Sebastian watched Noa's wonder, a sense of guilt and heartache gnawing at his soul.

"Noa," he said finally, breaking him out of his trance. "Can we discuss something?"

"Um, sure. What's up?"

Sebastian pulled him aside, away from the tourists that had gathered despite the chilly weather to observe the Falls. They sat down on a park bench, obscured from onlookers by evergreen trees.

"Are you okay?" Noa asked, a bit nervously. "You're acting weird today."

Sebastian ran a hand through his hair with a brief nod. "Everything is fine. Unless, of course, it's not. That is the constant state of our existence."

Noa just stared at him. He had never seen him so unraveled.

"Alright," Sebastian conceded. "I'm going to ask you a question and I implore you to answer honestly."

"Okay?" Noa watched the Niagara Co. boss apprehensively. If he had some kind of intel on the agent's undercover identity or his ties to CSIS, it certainly did not seem like it.

"Good." Sebastian drew in a deep breath. "Now, you've mentioned to me before that the persistent mess in your apartment is because you had absent parents and never learned to clean. You also told Elli when you met her that you came here from overseas on an exchange program, wanting to escape a family that treats you poorly." He paused. "Is this 'family' that you left abroad actually an orphanage?"

Noa listened to the question with confusion, thinking through the consequences of answering sincerely and Sebastian's potential motivations for asking. On the one hand, telling him could be dangerous in case the knowledge leads to deducing his placement at CSIS. On the other, the school has no right to disclose that information, and none of it is online.

After the split second it took him to consider his options, Noa answered, "Yeah. But it's a really small Catholic one, so I didn't think to mention it," he added, half-truthfully.

Sebastian weaved his fingers together, looking down to the gravel at their shoes. In a faint voice, he asked, "Is it called 'St. Isidore?'"

"It is!" Noa said, surprised. "How do you know? It's very obscure."

Sebastian kept his head down. "Yes, it is."

Noa furrowed his brows, a feeling of uneasiness creeping up again. "Why are you asking me this? If you know about Isidore's, then... you must have some kind of connection to them."

He stood from the bench, facing Sebastian.

"If you know that *I'm* from Isidore's, then you must have some kind of connection... to me..." his voice trailed off. "Where did you go yesterday?"

Sebastian looked up, a sorrowful expression flittering across his features. "Monaco."

Now it was Noa's turn to study Sebastian's face. "You *know* me." His tone was both uncertain and accusatory.

Sebastian fought the urge to look away. "Yes. We met before, when you were still called November. I should have realized it was you sooner. The fiery hair, the freckles. You must be, what, sixteen now? Seventeen?"

Noa shook his head, "Wait. But that can't... wait."

"When Elli told me that you're addicted to Tetris," Sebastian said with a dry laugh, "the pieces fell into place, so to speak. After all these years, you still play that game."

Noa's breath snagged hold on something inside his chest. He understood all at once why those icy eyes had put him off the first time they met. Bright and familiar; the color of the sky reflected in a mountain lake. He recognized them.

His head filled with fog as he covered his mouth with both hands. "No. You can't be him. You can't be September," he said, taking a step back.

Sebastian gave a slight, shameful nod. "September, Misha, whichever—"

"No!" Noa cried out furiously, drawing the attention of

passersby from the park trails around them. "Don't say his *name!*"

Stunned by the sudden outburst, Sebastian stood as well. "Noa, please believe me. What do you want me to say? I can tell you about Sister Ingrid or Father Emilio, or about the secret stash of chocolate I showed you in our room—"

"Stop!" Noa took another step back, his eyes welling up with tears. "You... you're an impostor. You're not September! You can't be, because September's dead!"

"*What?*" Sebastian pinched the bridge of his nose. "Of course. Of course, they would tell you that. Anything except for the truth."

The truth. Noa shuddered, trying to back away more but finding himself pressed against a fir instead. "This can't be happening," he whispered, then raised his voice again. "September died. They told me! He found out what I did and ran back to Russia and died!"

"No, no," Sebastian held his hands out slowly, taking a careful step forward. "I promise you, that's not what happened."

"Why should I believe you?!" Noa cried. "You barely even look like him!"

Sebastian took another tentative step. "Noël."

Noa shut his eyes, burying his hands in his hair. "No! You... you can't be..." he slid down against the tree, collapsing to the ground.

"Please listen," Sebastian said softly, crouching beside him. "I had to leave because of what they did to my friend. The November that preceded you. I was worried that the same fate awaited you if I stayed, so I had to run."

The redhead didn't respond, his posture limp against the evergreen.

"I didn't have much time," Sebastian said, "but I did leave you a note. In the hidden floorboard."

Noa glanced up, eyes wet with tears. "I couldn't, um. I never opened it after he— after you... well, you know. Died. Left. Whatever."

Sebastian scoffed. "Right, that makes sense. Maybe it's still there."

"What did it say?"

"I forget the details, as it was over ten years ago now," Sebastian said, remembering. "I apologized for leaving you in that awful place on your own. And told you that if you wanted to meet again, I would wait for you every New Year's Eve at St. Basil's Cathedral after your twelfth birthday. If I recall, that was the—"

"The Tetris loading screen," Noa mumbled, hiding his face in his hands. "You flew to Moscow every year for five years?"

Sebastian smiled, sitting down against the tree beside Noa. "I have the ticket stubs to prove it, if you don't believe me."

Noa was trembling. "So, you... You didn't leave because of me? Because of what I..."

"Whatever they told you; whatever they made you believe, it was a lie," Sebastian said, wrapping an arm around Noa reflexively. "I promise, I don't know anything about your past before St. Isidore, and I don't need to."

The relief that washed over Noa was immeasurable. The world around him caved in and faded away into a flood of forgotten memories and the distant crashing of the Niagara Falls.

"I'm so, so sorry," Sebastian said quietly. "I have so much to tell you, but all that can wait. Just know that I will not abandon you again."

In this moment, nothing else existed except this promise.

The investigation, the insider trading, the safe. Everything fell away, replaced by a gentle nothingness and the comfort of this familiar embrace.

There were no words left to say.

TEN
ST. ISIDORE – PART VIII. UP IN SMOKE

- Cambridge, United Kingdom. December 2001 -

It was a quiet evening in the Cambridgeshire Constabulary.

Detective Sergeant Campbell held two coffees in her hands, awaiting the Detective Inspector. It was her first week back on the job after maternity leave, and she was grateful for a few days free of any major disturbances.

But a few hours ago, a number of residents in Eynesbury, about 10 miles away, reported a house ablaze and screaming from inside. Two bodies were recovered, an adult male and female, one of whom had already perished and the other died en route to the hospital.

The only survivor, presumably their son, was treated for mild smoke inhalation and subsequently brought to the constabulary as investigators raced to ascertain the cause.

DS Campbell watched the boy through the window of the waiting room from outside, heart swelling with pity.

"Looks like we're burning the midnight oil once again, eh, Jules?" Detective Inspector Bloom joined her, taking one of the coffee cups. "Is that for me? 'Ta."

Campbell gave a brief nod. "Shouldn't we take him to the hospital? Or his grandparents'? Poor boy must be devastated. He can't be older than four or five."

DI Bloom sipped the coffee with a sympathetic shrug. "The paramedics said he's fine. As for folks – neighbors say the family had none. In fact, constables on the scene said their landlady claimed no knowledge of a child at all."

"That's so odd," the other detective muttered. "Alright, well. With all due respect, I know I've only just returned, but could I lead?"

Bloom chuckled. "I'll choose not to take offense to that. Knock yourself out."

"Thank you," Campbell said, taking a breath. "Do we have any reports from the scene? His name?"

"Ash or Rivera should have the medical examiner's report to us as soon as it's ready," Bloom said with a glance at the clock. "As for his name, neighbors couldn't confirm but the mother, Claire, had a small Christmas tree tattoo on her side with 'Noël' written underneath and the date 11-11-1997."

"Noël," DS Campbell repeated to herself. "Just four years old."

"You sure you're ready, Jules?" Bloom asked with concern. "I can do this alone."

"No, no," Campbell put her hand on the doorknob. "We just need information, right? No problem. I'm okay."

"After you." DI Bloom followed DS Campbell inside, sitting down at the table in the bare interview room and powering on the recording machine in a swift, unnoticeable motion.

Across from them, a red-headed boy stared blankly at a cup of water held between his hands. They were mostly obscured by a jumper that was much too large for his tiny frame, but his fingers were slightly burned.

"Hi, darling," Campbell said softly, sitting down as well and placing her hands on the table in a display of good faith. "My name is Detective Sergeant Julie Campbell, but you can call me Jules. This is my partner, Detective Inspector Aria Bloom."

The boy paid no attention, steadfastly focused on his cup with large green eyes, partially hidden by tangled, flame-colored hair.

"What's your name, sweetheart?" Campbell asked gently. When no response came after some time, she added, "is it 'Noël?'"

He flinched.

The detective smiled. "That's a lovely name. Means Christmas in French, doesn't it? Do you speak French?"

Noël gripped the paper cup, shaking his head slightly. "My mum."

"Your mum's French?" DS Campbell glanced at her notes. Her voice softened again. "Noël, honey. Do you understand what's happened to you mum and dad?"

"Gone," he mumbled, head down. "In the fire."

"That's right," Campbell said. "I'm very sorry. DI Bloom and I just want to ask you a few questions about it, to figure out how the fire got started, okay?"

The boy stayed silent.

DS Campbell continued. "Did you see anybody start the fire? Your mum or your dad? A neighbor?"

He shook his head.

"The firefighters found you in the backyard. Were you outside when the fire started?" she asked.

He nodded.

DI Bloom raised a brow. "In December? Without a jacket? Why were you in the backyard, Noël?"

Flicking the edges of the paper cup, Noël hesitated. "In trouble," he said.

"Who was in trouble, sweetheart?" DS Campbell asked.

The boy didn't reply.

A short knock sounded at the door and a constable creaked it open, holding a folder. "Ma'am, we've just received the medical examiner's report and whatever SOCO could find," he said, handing it to DI Bloom.

She took the file with a 'thank you' and skimmed the contents as Campbell continued her line of questioning.

"Noël, did anybody come by to do repairs at your house recently? Did your dad do anything to the electric boxes around the home?"

He shook his head again.

Bloom nudged Campbell under the desk with her shoe, showing her a medical and coroner's report, careful to conceal any photos from the boy across the table.

Campbell cringed, then frowned, unable to hide her dismay. She leaned forward a bit. "Noël, were you in the backyard because you were in trouble? Did your dad do that to you a lot?"

Noël glanced up at her briefly. He nodded.

"Did he hurt your mum?" Campbell asked carefully.

"Yes," came the faint reply.

"Did he hurt you?"

"Sometimes."

DS Campbell inhaled sharply. "You're safe now, darling. He can't hurt you anymore."

DI Bloom gave her partner another light kick, motioning toward the door with her eyes.

"We'll be right back, okay?" Campbell said, pausing the tape. "Don't worry."

Once they stepped outside the interview room, Campbell slammed her half-full coffee into the rubbish bin.

"Can't believe this. First case back, and it's the fallout of an abusive father who tried to *incinerate* his wife and child? Just my luck," she grumbled.

"Breathe, Jules." Bloom leaned against the wall. "Not ideal, I know. But we don't know for sure it was the dad."

"What, you think the little boy did it? That's dark, even for you, Boss. Besides, the parameds and fire crew confirmed he was in the backyard and locked out from the inside."

"Fair enough," Bloom raised her hands. "But still, we can't rule out other suspects. Preliminary SOCO report shows that the cause was a circuit breaker overload."

Campbell folded her hands over her chest. "That happens in older houses, doesn't it? Was this an unfortunate accident?"

"I considered that, but the house is new," Bloom said. She checked the clock again. "Actually, Jules, you're probably right. About the father. Occam's razor, yeah?"

"That poor boy," Campbell sighed. "The write-up in his report... Can't believe someone could hurt their own child like that. I mean, that's downright branding. Unthinkable."

"Listen, why don't you call it a night?" Bloom offered. "I can wrap things up in here. Shauna from Social Services is on her way, so I'll just wait for her and get him ready."

"Oh, are you sure, ma'am?" her partner asked.

After a minute of convincing, DS Campbell thanked her boss and left with a wave, sadness lingering in her gaze as she took a final look at the interview room.

DI Bloom stepped back inside, closing the door. She

pressed a button on the tabletop machine and spoke into it. "Interview resumes at 23:51. Hi again, Noël. Just you and me, kiddo."

Noël had replaced fidgeting with the paper cup to fidgeting with the sleeve of his oversized jumper. He watched with some trepidation as DI Bloom sat down.

"You must be a smart kid," she said. "It's written in my file here that you like to play with computers. Take them apart, even."

Noël gave a half-shrug.

"You mum must have been pretty smart too," Bloom said. "And your dad."

"My mum," the boy said quickly. "Very smart."

"You loved your mum, yeah?" The detective inspector tapped a pen on the folder. "Did it make you mad when your dad hurt her?"

Noël clutched the edges of his sleeves tightly.

Bloom flipped to the second page in the folder. "My file also says the breakers in the house were tampered with, so that the circuits would overheat at a precise moment. Do you know what that means?"

No response.

The detective placed the report on the table. "It means mum and dad were murdered. The malfunction was timed. Whoever started this fire knew when it would begin."

No response.

"Noël," Bloom said patiently. "Listen. I understand. You don't need to hide it from me. Our scene-of-the-crime investigators found a red hair near the circuit breaker, caught behind a panel that didn't burn."

The boy's pallor grew noticeably as she went on.

"You couldn't take it anymore, yeah? The abuse. The burns. And you're smart for your age, gifted even." Bloom leaned in. "You timed it just right, trapping your dad *and your mum—*"

"No!" Noël interrupted in a shaky voice. "No, I didn't mean to!"

"You didn't mean to?" Bloom echoed. "All the evidence points to the contrary. You wanted to get rid of mum and dad, kiddo."

"No, no!" Eyes welling up, he buried his hands in his hair. "Not mum. She wasn't..."

"Aha. Mum was collateral damage, then?" DI Bloom sat back. "What happened tonight, hm? How did you do it?"

Tears streaked down Noël's face. "Mum wasn't... supposed to come home."

The detective nearly jumped when her cellphone rang in her pocket. "Jeez, can't get used to this thing," she muttered, answering the bulky device. "DI Bloom."

On the other end of the line, the Chief Superintendent told her that her interview needed to be destroyed immediately and that Shauna from Social Services would not be coming to pick up the boy from the fire.

Instead, someone would be flying in from out of town to take him to a Catholic orphanage specializing in gifted children with troubled pasts.

And that the blaze in Eynesbury was the result of an accidental electrical fault after all.

- Niagara Falls. Thursday, February 27, 2014 -

That evening, after sending a long apology text to Elli, Noa muted his phone and collapsed onto his bed. Emotionally drained, he stared up at the ceiling, trying to calibrate the day's revelations.

Sebastian Nové. September. Misha. *Misha.*

He still could not fully process the connection, although in hindsight, a lot of oddities about Sebastian started to make sense. His affinity for Russian books. His particular tastes for European chocolates. His Isidore-level intellect that got him this far in the mafia business.

Noa sat up suddenly.

Shit, he bit his lip, coming to two simultaneous realizations. One: his job, which was still ongoing. Two: now that Sebastian knew *he* was a St. Isidore alum, how would he explain his presence here?

Considering he didn't ask him anything about that earlier, did he think Noa ran like he did? Noa scratched at a vague itch on his nose. That could work. No way to verify that, because the school wouldn't confirm one way or another.

Okay, he thought, *one problem solved.* Pulling out his work computer from under the mattress, he noticed his hands were shaking. Noa placed the laptop in front of him, contemplating his next move.

This investigation meant so much to him, to his employers. He was so close to uncovering the truth.

And yet.

An ache in his chest manifested like a shroud of darkness, threatening to envelop his heart and swallow him whole.

Here was a chance to reunite with someone he thought he had lost. The possibility of losing Sebastian – of losing Misha – again sent pangs of nausea to his stomach.

What could he do? Sabotaging the investigation might get him arrested & extradited. Confessing to the Niagara Co. might get him killed.

He groaned in frustration, flipping open the laptop.

I need more time, he thought in dismay. *I'll come up*

with something later. I just need to throw them off Niagara's trail for now.

He kicked himself mentally for sending over those notes on all the members in the morning. Why couldn't he have just waited? *Oh,* he realized, *not* all *the members.*

Noa quickly powered up the internal chat system and sent off a series of messages to his boss.

```
[NS | 9:18 PM] hello sir
[NS | 9:18 PM] quick update I forgot to
include on the notes I sent earlier
[NS | 9:19 PM] you know how the one woman
always wears scarves
[NS | 9:19 PM] and you thought that might
be notable
[NS | 9:19 PM] it's not
[NS | 9:19 PM] I checked
[NS | 9:20 PM] under her scarf I mean
[NS | 9:20 PM] she took it off today and
there was nothing there
[NS | 9:20 PM] well I mean a normal neck
was there
[NS | 9:20 PM] no tattoos or scars or
whatever
[NS | 9:20 PM] anyway
[NS | 9:21 PM] that was all
[NS | 9:21 PM] have a good night
```

Noa shut the computer and lay back down. He hoped that would do the trick and at the very least, keep Lucy out of government custody. Even if she was a fugitive, he couldn't help but empathize with her situation and think she was better off here.

Unless she was the one that killed him if he was discovered. He shivered. He needed to think of a plan, and fast. If his situation was confusing before, now it was downright chaotic.

But he would do everything he could to keep his new family intact. Sebastian's promise echoed in his ears – *I will not abandon you again.*

Noa tried to call upon faded memories from their time at St. Isidore, forced into the dark caverns of his mind by less-than orthodox therapeutic sessions at the hands of Sister Ingrid. But he was there. Younger, and kinder, but Sebastian's face haunted those distant memories.

I will not abandon you again.

- Toronto. Friday, February 28, 2014 -

"Really, Alex? 8:00 in the morning?" Agent Lavoie yawned loudly, pouring herself a coffee in the back of the conference room.

"I'm sorry my *emergency meeting* was not timed conveniently for you, Miriam," Agent Koven said sarcastically, checking his watch. "Also, thank you for being punctual as always."

She curtsied, taking her seat beside Agent Sanders. Agent Lee rushed in soon after, grabbing a corner chair at the conference desk.

"Now that we're all here," Koven cleared his throat, "we can begin."

The ceiling projector illuminated the monitor in the

front of the room, displaying a series of screenshots, photos, and a map.

"Thank you for making it so promptly on such short notice," he said. "But as I stated in the memo, this is an emergency. I've already briefed the director last night, as soon as I became aware of the situation."

"Is this about the insider trading and Little Red?" Sanders asked. "I thought things were going smoothly down there."

Agent Koven looked downright morose. "This does concern Agent Sinclair. Tell me what you all make of this."

He zoomed into a screencap of messages.

Agent Lavoie slipped on her glasses and leaned forward, reading through the transcript half-aloud. *"That one woman... no tattoos or scars.* Hm. He's referring to NL-9009, I presume?"

"Yes," Koven confirmed. "But doesn't something strike you as odd about these messages?"

"You mean, other than the god-awful teenage typing?" Lavoie asked. "Well, it is a bit odd, I suppose. He told us about her military background before. That, combined with her location, apparent age, background, and consistent neck coverings all pointed to the Nano Laqueus."

"Also," Sanders chimed in, "why did he forget this in his notes? Why does he sound like he's typing it in a hurry?"

"Exactly," Koven said.

"If I may, sir." Lee said timidly. "Isn't all that evidence circumstantial at best? If he really did see her neck, then perhaps she is just a false flag?"

"There's one more thing." Koven flipped to an online news column. "A few weeks ago, Noa sent me this article about an explosion in New York, apparently orchestrated by the Niagara Co. and their rivals. He told me that he and the Niagara location team were present."

The others skimmed the article.

"This only mentions that five 'suspicious looking' individuals were there," Lee said. "And there aren't any photos."

Lavoie tapped her pen against the conference table. "But Alex figured there must have been security footage around the area of the exploded building, right? Every street corner, every alleyway."

"Precisely," he said, flipping to a blurry image of a woman in a scarf and a man in a white suit on the screen. "It isn't ideal, and the photos on record we have on NL-9009 are either corrupted or old, but based on this, I can say with about 95% confidence that this woman is the escaped subject."

"So then," Sanders frowned. "What are we supposed to make of those messages?"

Agent Koven's expression soured, even more so than before. "I believe Noa has been compromised and was forced to send these communications to throw us off NL-9009's trail. Therefore, as of last night, I have officially declared a Code 136."

Agent Lee's mouth fell open. "A hostage situation?"

"Please don't sound so excited, Thomas," Lavoie chastised. "Colson knows? What did she say?"

Koven nodded, bringing the presentation back to the map. "She knew this might be a risk, and we proceeded with the caveat that Noa's safe return would be prioritized if the NL subject posed a threat. Basically, we have to get him back. Any means necessary."

"I'm assuming you haven't responded," Lavoie said.

"Not yet," Koven confirmed. "I'll think of some way to

reply later this morning. For now, I pray they don't know that we know, and they will keep him alive."

"How can we infiltrate this early without letting Sinclair know?" Sanders asked.

Lavoie uncapped her pen. "I have some ideas."

ELEVEN
BETRAYAL

- Unknown Location. Saturday, March 1, 2014 -

Sebastian woke from a sleep he did not remember taking, to find himself in handcuffs.

He opened his eyes and regretted doing so immediately. The four white walls in the tiny room were blinding and, combined with the fluorescent lights, worsened his growing headache.

He brought one bound hand to his aching head, the other forced to follow. His lodgings consisted of roughly three-square meters, a bare bed, a table with three chairs, and a toilet. In the corner of the ceiling, a silver camera watched him silently.

Sebastian stood from the bed with a wince and walked the perimeter of his room. He glanced down at himself, noting that he had been searched and relieved of his suit jacket, watch, and everything in his pockets.

He sat in a chair and turned it to face the camera, staring into the lens dead-on.

And waited.

And waited.
And waited.

On the other end of the camera's transmission, watching the feed with professional curiosity, Agents Koven and Lavoie shared a box of donuts.

"Mm," Lavoie closed her eyes. "This is the first thing I ate since we touched down. Thank you."

Koven nodded absentmindedly, staring back at the pair of piercing blue eyes on the screen in contempt. "This may have been a mistake, Miriam. We searched everywhere – people are *still* searching – and Noa is nowhere to be found."

"Careful, Alex," she said, mouth full. "He might smell your fear."

"Hopefully we can get something out of him," Koven said. "You ready?"

Lavoie grabbed another donut. "Not yet. Let him stew a bit more."

"Right, that's what we're doing," Koven said.

"Knock, knock!" Two taps on the door preceded Director Colson peeking into their temporary office. "I heard we caught the big kahuna of the Niagara Co. Where, where?"

The two agents motioned to the live transmission.

"You're joking." The director stepped inside, taking a donut for herself. "*That's* the Sebastian Nové we've been chasing?"

Koven shrugged. "We assume so, ma'am. He matches Sinclair's description, and he introduced himself as such when we apprehended him. Strangely, he didn't seem surprised at all to see us."

The director peered at Sebastian through the screen. "Wow. Millennials are really taking *all* the jobs these days, aren't they?"

"He does seem young," Lavoie agreed. "But, if we're stuck here interrogating him, at least he's easy on the eyes," she added playfully.

Director Colson nudged her with an elbow. "Hey, can I have a go? I miss being in the field, and he really is so striking."

"Oh, sure, if you're into that show-off Wallstreet look," Koven muttered under his breath.

The director turned to him. "What was that, Alex?"

He just shook his head, shoving a half-eaten donut into his mouth. "Agent Lavoie and I should get started, ma'am."

"Before you go," she said, "I wanted to tell you two that I received a call from the office of the Attorney General about ten minutes ago. Once we're ready to prosecute, Juliette Mercer wants the case."

"No pressure, huh?" Lavoie said sarcastically, glancing at the screen. "Guess we better get started."

The sealed white cell door slid open with an automated hiss.

Sebastian pivoted himself in the chair to face the two newcomers that entered the small space – a man and a woman. They wore sharp suits and an unfamiliar emblem on their lapel pins and badges. An explosion of blue swords surrounding a red maple leaf, atop which sat a gold encrusted crown decorated with the fleur-de-lis.

A brief expression of confusion flickered across Sebastian's face as he came to realize he was in Canadian custody.

The door slid closed once more and the agents took their seats across from him.

Sebastian watched them silently. The woman, seated on the left, crossed her arms across her chest and shot him a brief, insincere smile. Her light brown hair was packed neatly in a bun and designer glasses rested on the bridge of her nose.

On the right beside her, the other agent offered no friendly gestures, however ingenuine. A dark-haired man, serious and stoic, he was borderline glaring across the table.

Both appeared to be somewhere in their mid-to-late thirties, and both were armed.

The male agent spoke first. "State your name for the record, and your affiliation with the Niagara Company."

Sebastian raised a brow. "That's your opening statement? I already told you, and the gentlemen that were with you earlier. And then, it would appear, they subsequently knocked me out. I thought Canadians were known for their good manners?"

"Our good manners are reserved for good people," the female agent said wryly. "We know what you said. We just found it hard to believe that a *child* such as yourself would possess the means to lead a criminal empire." She placed a heavy emphasis on the key word. "We were afraid you were merely a pawn; a red herring set up for us to detain."

"Frankly, I don't care what you believe," Sebastian responded, glancing at the badge on her belt, "Madame Lavoie. But I am curious as to what Canadian Intelligence wants with me."

"Are you now? We're curious about some things as well," the other agent said with some disdain. "For instance, you knew that we were coming. You cleared the place out in advance and were expecting us. And yet, you claim not to know the reason for your being here. That strikes me as odd. Doesn't it seem odd, Miriam?"

"Very," Lavoie nodded. "I wonder why that is."

Sebastian didn't respond.

- Niagara Falls. Friday morning, February 28 -

The day after his reunion with Noa, Sebastian could hardly focus.

Between the plans for a relocation to a new office, the fallout with Nick's contacts in the West, and a third straight day without adequate sleep, his thoughts swirled in a jumbled mess.

A lingering suspicion kept him awake, despite his delight at finding Noa again.

Why did he, a student of St. Isidore, come here? Asking for a job at an ice cream shop? And why did he ask so many questions?

Sebastian never did get the chance to ask if he ran away. Yesterday did not seem like the right time to bring up more talk of St. Isidore. He supposed he ought to give Noa the benefit of the doubt. After all, he had passed the initiation. And Sebastian was plagued by the guilt of knowing his absence impacted Noa's life so negatively in that dreadful orphanage.

Operating on autopilot, he slid his hand along the hidden panel on the wall and entered a combination into the lock. As the safe popped open, he found himself admitting once again how much this office lacked natural light. He desperately yearned to open a window.

Although not a top priority, he had set his sights now on

a new, multi-story office location in Niagara-on-the-Lake. Close enough to the Falls' underground, but far enough away from the current space and across the border, he planned to relocate gradually before connecting the subterranean pathways.

Tossing the Newspaper onto his desk, as per his morning routine before the stock markets opened at 9:30, Sebastian momentarily skimmed the front page for any economic turbulence or major news.

His body froze as he caught sight of the main spread headline.

Old York T

Saturday, March 1, 2014

Great Lakes Drug Bust

A Niagara-based subdivision of the locally infamous Great Lakes Collective was busted today for trading cocaine, methamphetamine, & fentanyl, authorities said. The New York State police, who patrolled both sides of the border at locations of interest in partnership with the RCMP for the past five months, were able to make one arrest.

The arrest came after undercover detectives netted 10 kilograms of cocaine, 60 kilograms of crystal methamphetamine, and more than 800 grams of fentanyl, authorities said.

The NYSP launched the investigation after civilians complained about suspicious traffic from potential drug dealers. State Trooper Jim Milligan and New York DA Michelle Brown announced that the bust resulted in the arrest of one subdivision leader, that of the Niagara Company, known locally as Don Nové. More detail regarding prosecution to follow.

He exhaled a slow, restrained breath.

"Shit."

Upstairs, at the Polar Parlor, Noa dropped a second cone of ice cream to the floor.

"You good, 'hon?" Elli spun around, concerned. "Some of our customers are short but not to that extent."

Noa cleaned it up hastily, apologizing. "My bad, Elli! Sorry. I just, um. I'm out of it today."

"You've been out of it a lot recently!" She gave the waiting patrons a fresh cone and sent them on their way. "What's on your mind?"

He wiped some ice cream from his apron, keeping his hands occupied. "Can I get your opinion on something?"

Elli perked up, taking a seat on the counter. "Sure! What's up?"

"Well, I have this friend," Noa said tentatively. "Overseas. He's the one with the problem."

She nodded, "Go on."

"He's having trouble choosing between a job with incredible career prospects and his, um, family." Noa searched for the right words. "Basically, he has to choose between keeping a job that is really good but detrimental to those he cares about… versus losing that job and also risking his future to avoid hurting them. What would be your advice— to my friend?"

"That's easy, sugar," Elli said. "You can't put a price on family. No job is worth more than the people we care about! Trust me, I learned the hard way." She placed her hands on the counter, leaning back. "Jobs are replaceable, hon'. The people we love are not."

Finding comfort in her words, Noa nodded to himself. "Right. I'll pass that along."

"But after you get a new apron, right?" Elli said with a lighthearted smile. "Go grab one from the back. And see what Mike is doing, rummaging around in there."

"Yes, ma'am!" Tension eased, Noa made his way to the staff-only door. He would do it. He would come clean. Soon. As soon as he could muster up the courage and a proper explanation, he would tell them everything.

Noa opened the back door, nearly hitting Mike in the head.

"Oh – careful kiddo!" He was kneeling by a number of half-packed boxes, stuffing them hastily with paperwork.

A series of cardboard and plastic boxes in varying sizes stood by the staircase to the second floor as well, near the entrance to the concealed elevator.

"What's going on?" Noa asked, setting his ice cream-stained apron aside.

Mike straightened up, cracking his neck. "Didn't I tell you and El'? Shoot, maybe I forgot to do that when I came up here." He scratched at his chin. "I thought I did though."

"Are we moving?" Noa concluded on his own.

"Well, yeah, that's old news," Mike said. "Apparently the Boss's current setup doesn't have enough windows. But as of this morning, we're movin' ahead of schedule. All essentials and non-storage goods are goin' to the new place."

"Ahead of schedule?" Noa repeated. "How far ahead? When's the move?"

Mike wiped some sweat off his brow. "By the end of the day."

Having read over the article more times than he could bear, Sebastian was certain of two key facts:

1. Someone had double-crossed him, and
2. He needed to evacuate his team immediately.

Concerning the first issue, his thoughts first jumped to Noa. But upon some consideration, he reckoned that the Newspaper actually absolved him of suspicion. Sure, Noa's presence was questionable at best, but the story referenced a 5-month long investigation, while Noa had only been with the team for about a month.

Also, the teen had not been involved in any Niagara Co. trades, so how could he have fed this information to state troopers?

Sebastian paced the floor of his office, which felt more claustrophobic by the minute. How could he have missed the involvement of state law enforcement on this scale? And on something as petty as drugs?

Since receiving the Newspaper, and even some time before that, he had shifted his focus away from the day-to-day operations, focusing instead on the larger financial and expansion strategies. Perhaps that was the problem. He had to admit, the amounts of narcotics quoted did not align with his recollection, but then again, Nick kept that inventory.

Not that he could ask. *Hey, Nick, could you check this fortune-telling paper?* He scoffed.

It didn't matter, anyway.

The Newspaper was no vague, prophetic vision, appearing to him in a fever dream. It had proven itself to be accurate, time and time again. It could anticipate the most unpredictable, untamable of economic beast and it saved him from certain death more than once. And if it said his arrest was imminent, he knew it must be so.

Still, the future would not happen on its own. The safety of his team was Sebastian's top priority. Even if one of them – could it be Nick, he thought? Certainly not Mike or Elli – might have betrayed him, he still had to get them to a new location. Especially Lucy, who would face lifetime containment, or death, if captured.

Hastily, but with care to ensure no damage, Sebastian packed the Newspaper into a cardboard box with an assortment of random documents and office items. He called Mike in and informed him of an update to their moving plans: expedited to today.

The Niagara-on-the-Lake office would have to do.

He glanced around his office, mostly empty from a few hours of haphazard packing. He couldn't stand the thought of a plan left unfinished, and the prospect of an arrest was less than appealing, but better him than his team. And he knew Elli would do what's necessary in his absence.

In any case, with his long-standing connections in New York, he did not plan on staying arrested for long. He would keep his promise. He would not lose another November.

When the New York State Troopers would show up on Saturday to make their arrest, Sebastian would ensure he was the only one present.

- Toronto. Friday afternoon, February 28 -

The 18th floor conference room had filled up with a small task force of CSIS agents as Agent Koven positioned himself in front of a whiteboard, crowded with maps, arrows, and notes.

"Okay, Agent Sinclair disclosed the two locations he was investigating: a winery and an ice cream store in Niagara Falls. We haven't been able to trace any of his devices – he's surprisingly good at keeping them off – but thanks to a corporate credit card purchase at a nearby shopping mall, we're sure he's somewhere in the area."

As Koven said this, he circled them on a large map of the Niagara region with a red marker.

"Sanders and Lee: you're on Little Italy. Take Sanchez's team and start with the Bella Luna. Miriam and I will take the rest of you and cover the ice cream shop near the border on Old Falls."

The others in the room, some sitting, some standing, took note and nodded intermittently.

"Our primary objective," Koven added, "is locating and safely retrieving Agent Sinclair. The secondary objective, if possible, is the arrest and apprehension of the Niagara Company's members. At this time, we are only able to confirm the appearance of two – you can find them in the briefing memo. The rest are description-based."

Agent Lee raised his hand. "Are you sure this is enough people, sir?" He looked around the conference room. "Aren't we potentially setting off a mafia war?"

Koven straightened his tie uncomfortably. "This is as much as we're authorized. I should also mention that this mission is strictly confidential. No one breathes a word of it outside these walls."

A rumble of murmurs rippled through the small crowd.

Agent Sanchez spoke up. "Is the agency accountable here if we screw up? I mean, with this underage agent kidnapped and you being the cause?"

"Thank you for your input, Carmen," Lavoie said with false politeness. "I can personally assure you that if you screw up, the right people will know."

Sanchez held her tongue.

Placing the marker back on the board, Agent Koven cleared his throat. "That's all for now. Once we work out the logistics, we'll set off across the border." He checked his watch. "Hopefully in a few hours. Miriam – sidebar?"

Lavoie followed him to the far window, giving the two of them enough distance from the others in the large conference room to speak privately.

She retrieved her cellphone from her blazer pocket, checking it quickly. "Ah, *bon*," she smiled to herself. "The Times is on board."

Koven shook his head slightly in disbelief. "Just like that?"

"I have good connections," she said. "So, what shall they print? With the Star, Globe, and Times, all the regional news will follow. Falls Gazette, York Tribune, whatever. And by the time TV media picks it up, I'm hoping we'll have something real to give them."

"You've done this before, haven't you?" Koven asked.

"Done what, Alex?"

He chuckled. "I'm impressed, and a bit afraid. Here I am, eaten away by guilt and panic at the mere prospect of tricking the public with a cover up. And then there's you."

Lavoie patted him on the arm, slipping her phone back into her pocket. "This is why you lose to me at chess, every time. Think: what would happen otherwise? If civilians found out that we've been sitting on information about a murderous government experiment walking around the streets of an idyllic tourist town. And for what? Some intelligence on market trading?"

"You're right," he sighed. "And admitting that this international fugitive is holding one of our agents hostage – a child, no less – would do irreparable damage to our reputation. How do we even explain someone like Noa working for us?"

"We don't," she said with a smirk. "We write our own version of events. What'll it be? Guns? Drugs? Gambling? I think New York State Police will be believable. Maybe Mounties."

Koven looked out the window with a frown and thought for a long time. "Drugs. We can take the most recent numbers we know got trafficked across the Rainbow Bridge and inflate them a bit. Say it was a joint operation."

"Bon," she said. "I'll get my press guys on it."

- Niagara-on-the-Lake. Saturday morning, March 1 -

A calm, misty sunrise crept over the serene streets of the small lakefront town.

"Alright, I'll admit," Nick said, pushing the door to a vacant office open with his side and stepping into the large, bright room. "This place is kinda nice."

He placed a cardboard box down to the floor, making room for Mike, who was straining under the weight of a temporary fish tank.

"Phew! It'll be even nicer when it's all set up." Mike placed the tank against a wall.

Noa set two bulky suitcases beside it, as well as his backpack. "Did Sebastian tell you guys why we had to move so soon? We didn't even decide what to do with the Polar Parlor."

"Eh, he only lets us in on his plans about half the time," Nick shrugged. "The better question is, where is he and the rest of 'em? My back won't forgive me for this."

Mike checked his watch. "The girls are out gettin' breakfast at Maria's; they should be here soon. I asked Lucy to bring us some of those Russian crepes they're always ravin' about. And the Boss mentioned he needed to move the *Aurora* upriver."

"Classic," Nick scoffed. "We move the boxes; he moves the yacht."

Noa perked up. "There's a yacht?"

"Oh, you haven't seen the *Aurora* yet?" Mike gasped in faux surprise. "The jewel of the Great Lakes! The splendor of the seas! The Boss's one and only precious baby."

Nick chuckled. "So precious, he's upgraded it three times already. Calls it the Cruiser Aurora. She's a fine boat, but a bit flashy for my tastes."

"Do you think I can see it?" Noa asked excitedly.

"Yeah, why not, kiddo?" Mike said with a grin. "When the Boss gets here, we should take her out for a spin on the lake."

- Niagara Falls. Saturday, March 1, 2014 -

At around the same time that morning, three miles away on the other side of the border, three unmarked vehicles pulled up to the intersection of Old Falls and 1st Street. Men and women in dark, plain clothes assembled in front of the Polar Parlor, awaiting instruction.

Agents Koven and Lavoie directed a few of their team members to keep civilians away from the area and met up with a skeleton crew by the front door.

"Alright, Simms and Paolo, go around the back," Koven said in a hushed voice. "The rest of us will enter through the front."

Lavoie peered up, shielding her eyes from the sun. "Cute place. You don't really think they operate from an ice cream shop, do you?"

"Check out the sign," Agent Simms said, pointing to a sticker on the window.

A white bear in a Polar Parlor apron, with a 'Pecan'

nametag, proudly exclaimed, *Attention to Detail, Commitment to Quality* in a snowy speech bubble.

"Hm. Coincidence?" Lavoie shrugged. "Maybe I could grab a sundae for later, what do you think, Alex?"

Koven held out a hand with an urgent hush. "I think someone's inside. Secure the perimeter."

"Yessir!" Agents Simms and Paolo hurried to the back of the Parlor, as a few junior agents flanked Koven and Lavoie's sides.

Lavoie peered into the glass, past the hanging snowflakes and early St. Patrick's Day decorations. "Are you sure? It's not even 8 o'clock."

"Come on," Koven said, preparing his gun.

"It's an ice cream shop, Alex," his partner teased, opening the door with a welcoming jingle. "Oh, it's unlocked. Hello?"

Koven followed, staying close to her side. The shop seemed recently vacated from within – most of the display desserts had been removed, and the chalkboard menu-of-the-week had been erased. A massive aquarium spanning the length of the western wall stood empty.

The agent frowned, hand still hovering over his gun. "They knew we were coming, Miriam."

"How?" She whispered, "that's impossible."

From behind the counter, a bear-shaped robot thrummed to life with a series of mechanical beeps.

In a conditioned response, the two agents whipped out their weapons and aimed them at the machine.

"What the hell is that?" Koven said, taken aback.

The bot, unaware of the danger, proceeded to gather two scoops of ice cream and load them onto waffle cones.

As the agents watched in bewilderment, a well-dressed

young man popped up from behind the counter, holding a remote.

"Ah, good morning," he said politely. "You'll have to excuse the PecanBot. You see, we're a bit short-staffed at the moment. Could I interest you in some dessert?"

The agents shifted their aim from the ice cream bot to its master, exchanging a knowing glance.

"Hands where we can see them," Koven commanded. "Identify yourself! Who are you?"

He held up his hands with a bored expression. "Sebastian Nové. Let's get this over with."

From behind him, the employee door swung open. Agent Simms darted inside, training his weapon on Sebastian as well.

"Sir, ma'am – the back is completely cleared out. And the office upstairs is empty too."

Sebastian looked to Agents Koven and Lavoie impatiently. "You can put the firearms away, officers. I'll cooperate fully."

- Unknown location. Saturday, March 1, 2014 -

It wasn't often that Sebastian found himself perplexed.

Once in a while, sure, he might be stumped by a strange cultural difference or perhaps thrown off by the bizarre choices made by those he dealt with in the criminal trade.

But such a profound feeling of confusion? He was unaccustomed to its overwhelming intrusion of his usually put-together way of life. It was exceedingly unpleasant.

The paper clearly stated New York State Police. These people were not State troopers.

Was the Newspaper mistaken? He thought, headache intensifying. *It had never been wrong before.* Lost in thought, Sebastian inattentively heard one of the agents speaking.

"How did you know we were coming?" Agent Koven demanded, a second time now.

Sebastian pressed a hand to his forehead, unsure how to respond. "I didn't."

"That's bull," Koven said bluntly. "The shop and the office above it had been cleaned out, as if you had been expecting us."

"I wasn't expecting *you*, per se," Sebastian replied under his breath.

Agent Lavoie's cellphone chirped with a text notification, which she ignored, while tapping her foot restlessly. "I'm not sure we're getting anywhere, Alex."

"Just tell us where he is, damn it," Koven said. "Save us all some time."

Plagued by confusion yet again, Sebastian frowned. "Who?"

Lavoie's phone chirped again. She glanced at it briefly, before sliding it back into her blazer pocket. "No need to play dumb," she said. "You said you would co-operate, so co-operate! We searched everywhere."

"I assure you, I am not playing at anything," Sebastian said, his frustration growing. "I would appreciate it if you told me why I'm here, where 'here' is, and what, exactly, you want from me."

Koven, just about ready to burst, clenched his fists. "Where is Noa Sinclair, you son of a bitch?!"

Like a punch to the gut, the agent's words stole all the air from his body. Sebastian drew a sharp breath, sensing the oppressively bright, white walls start to close in around him.

"You're looking for... Noa?" His voice was tense, cold.

Agent Lavoie leaned over to her partner, lowering her voice. "Alex, I think he didn't know about Red."

Agent Koven watched the young man before him, previously composed, recede into a vacant-eyed shell.

"Hm," Koven's brows knitted together in thought. "I think you might be right. This is certainly a turn for the strange."

Sebastian stared at the cement floor. The traitor was Noa after all.

"Doesn't change the fact that we need to get him back," Lavoie said, ignoring another two notification tones from her blazer pocket. "So, out with it, Mr. Nové. Where is our agent?"

He didn't respond. Noa's betrayal was secondary to the safety of his team members.

Koven sighed indignantly. "Come on. You don't want to keep him around any base of operations for too long – the kid's a genius. If not for this hiccup, I'm certain he would've figured out your insider trading tricks in a matter of weeks."

Sebastian let out a joyless chuckle. "*That's* what you sent him to investigate?"

The agent retrieved a folded-up piece of paper from his breast pocket. "He kept note of all sorts of information. Your financial consultant, 'Elli,' might we find her on Wall Street since she was not at the Polar Parlor? Oh, and apologies for not giving Noa a heads up about Benetti's ex. Probably caused you some unnecessary trouble. How's the burn, by the way? The explosion must've left a nasty scar."

Lavoie shook her head at her partner's delight from inflicting such torture on their captive. He went on.

"Quite a lot about you," he said with a slight smirk. "What's your favorite bit, Miriam? Personally, the part about the chocolate and old Russian literature was mine."

Lavoie peered at the notes. "Gosh, Red's handwriting is atrocious. I like 'definitely manages insider trading.'"

"Yeah, that's a good one, too," Koven agreed.

Every word made Sebastian's skin crawl. They knew so much. Too much. Because of Noa. Because he let Noa get too close.

The headache had mutated into a migraine and he could hardly hear them now.

Koven folded the paper back up, putting it away. "Tell us where he is."

Hoarsely, Sebastian managed to reply, "No."

Lavoie finally checked the messages on her phone, scrolling through them with passive interest. "What a shame. I suppose we could try our luck with the fugitive woman."

"What?!" Sebastian's head shot up, an action that sent pain surging down his neck.

"We didn't tell you?" Koven said, standing from the chair. "The team that searched your winery apprehended your pal Lucy. Also known as NL-9009."

"No," Sebastian said to himself, "that can't be true."

Lavoie stood too, transfixed by a message on her phone. "One last thing," she said, glancing at him with a peculiar glimmer in her eyes. "Is that your natural hair color?"

He barely registered her voice, but the question pierced through his haze intrusively. *"What did you say?"*

"Never mind." She smiled and pressed her mobile to her chest, taking her leave with Agent Koven. "See you soon, I'm sure."

The cell door slid shut behind them and locked with a mocking click.

Agent Koven sat in one of the command room chairs with a heavy sigh, reaching over a video operating board for a stale donut.

"I don't get it," he said after a few irritated bites. "If Noa wasn't held hostage by NL-9009, whom we've captured, and he didn't break his cover with the Niagara Co., then, where is he? He hasn't responded to my messages yet. And why the hell is this guy covering for him?"

Agent Lavoie, leaning against a desk of monitors, held her cellphone out for her partner to see. "I have a hunch," she said, a sly smile growing at the corners of her mouth.

Koven squinted at the small screen. "Why are you showing me a photo of children, Miriam?"

"*Tsk*, pay attention, Alex," she said. "Don't you recognize any of these kids?"

He took the cellphone from her hands, zooming into the photograph. "Is that Noa? The little redheaded one in the bottom row?"

Lavoie nodded, pleased with herself. "Cute, right? So small."

"How did you get this?" Koven gaped at her. "Why did you?"

She took the device back, moving to sit beside him. "I just reached out to the people that sent Colson the file about Sinclair. I figured, in case he's missing, we would need pictures of his face, and we don't have any. When I chatted them up in French, they were quite friendly. But they didn't have any portrait shots; only these group photos."

"Right," Koven said with a slight frown. "That makes sense. If he's missing, I mean. Good call."

"Yeah, yeah," she waved off the compliment. "Look at this, though," she said excitedly, handing him the phone again. "This is the first group photo they have of our little Noa. Taken when he first arrived at the orphanage or school or whatever it is."

Koven studied the picture. "And? I see Noa there; he's the second last one."

"Right," she said. "But look closer. Anyone else familiar?"

He furrowed a brow, zooming in again. "I'm bad with faces," he said. "Who should I be focusing on?"

Lavoie used her finger to move the zoom over, pointing at a teenager two spots to the left of Noa.

"The blond?" Koven asked, squinting at the screen again. "Why?" He inspected the photo for a few moments. "Wait. You don't think that's Nové?"

He looked at her, baffled, then to the video transmission screen of the cell.

"Holy shit," he breathed. "It is."

"Are we being played, Alex?" Lavoie leaned back, crossing her arms.

"I don't know," he said in earnest. "What does it mean? Could they be— oh, hang on. That's Sanders' team calling." He turned to a separate visual feed, which sprang to life when he answered its beeping tone.

"Sir! Ma'am!" Sanders blurted out once the audio connected. "Can you hear me? We've been trying to get a signal for ten minutes."

"We hear you," Koven said, lowering the volume. "What's going on? Where are you?"

"You'll never believe this, sir," Sanders said eagerly. "We're underground!"

The video feed spun around, displaying a narrow, windowless access tunnel lined with a few metal doors.

Lavoie removed her glasses, rubbing the bridge of her

nose. "Wonderful. Another fun surprise. No sign of our missing child, I presume?"

"We're still searching, ma'am," Sanders said. "We discovered this place by accident. After Sanchez took the woman with the scarf away, Lee and I stayed behind at the Bella Luna to see what we could find."

Agent Lee popped up on the screen. "It's quite incredible, ma'am! I wanted to grab a few Niagara ice wines from their stockroom for my girlfriend, and one of the bottles unlocked a hidden access elevator."

"Put the evidence back, Lee." Koven turned to Lavoie. "That can't be legal, right? I mean, building permit-wise?"

"I'm sure that's the least of their concerns," she said. "How far does it extend?"

"Far," Sanders responded, "and deep. We've only cleared a few floors so far. No sign of Sinclair yet."

"We're five floors below ground now," Lee added. "There's some kind of rumbling in the distance so that's where we've been heading."

Koven nodded, the lines on his forehead creasing with worry. "Roger that. Be careful."

The agents in the control room watched the monitor, increasingly uneasy, as the sound of muffled thunder permeated through the transmission audio. Sanders and Lee pressed on, carefully navigating a winding hall with readied weapons.

After a few minutes, they entered a large, rounded chamber. The rumbling above them swelled into a booming, sending rippling vibrations across the computer's speakers. Sanders panned the camera across, showing a series of doors lining the curving wall.

"Do you see what we see?" he asked, raising his voice over the noise in the hall.

"Yes," Koven said, "but what are we looking at? 'Goat?' 'Bird?' 'Bridal Veil?'"

Lavoie seized his shoulder with a gasp. "The waterfalls. See, those doors say 'Canada' and 'America.' That sound – you guys are under the Niagara Falls."

Koven gave a nervous laugh. "No way. Right? They couldn't have built beneath the falls. That's crazy."

"Actually, sir, I think Agent Lavoie is correct," Lee said, gazing upwards. "Judging by the distance we walked from the elevator and the Bella Luna's location, we should be standing atop the Niagara River right now."

Sanders walked over to the door labeled 'Bridal Veil' apprehensively. "Probably shouldn't use explosives to bust these open then."

"Jesus," Koven muttered. "The hell are they keeping down there? Can you open any of the doors?"

Lee crouched by the lock to the room labeled 'Canada.' "I can give it a shot."

From behind the camera, Sanders, as well as Koven and Lavoie, waited in anticipation as the agent worked on the bolted mechanism of the door.

Temporarily muting their audio, Lavoie tapped a nail against the screen of her cellphone. "Should we give a status update to Colson?"

"And say what?" Koven raked his fingers through his hair. "We still haven't found Noa. We still don't know how Nové conducts the insider trading. Hell, we can't even connect him to it with non-circumstantial evidence. Best we can pin on him is a building code violation."

"I suppose you're right," Lavoie conceded. "I doubt Attorney Mercer will care that they grew up at the same orphanage, either."

"Likely not," Koven said, stretching his back. "It *would*

help the prosecution's case if we could get real evidence connecting Niagara Co. to their crimes."

"Sir? Ma'am? Can you hear us?" Agent Lee, waving to Sanders' visual transmission, shouted enthusiastically. "It's open!"

Koven unmuted the mic. "We're here. Proceed with caution."

With a nod, Lee carefully pushed the door open.

"Goddamn," Sanders exhaled behind the camera. "That's a lot of firearms."

Leaning in for a better view of the display, Koven whistled. "How's that for evidence?"

Lavoie removed her glasses, giving them a quick wipe on her blouse before putting then on again. "*Crisse*," she said under her breath. "That will do, yes."

Lee approached a stack of rifles, piled neatly on shelves along the wall. "There must be hundreds in here," he said. "And ammo stored separately in these crates below. They're all just marked 'Deadhorse.'"

"What's written above the shelf, Lee?" Koven asked, trying to make out the detail.

"Labels, sir," Lee said. "This one says 'St. Lawrence' and the rifle stack beside it is labelled 'Rideau.'"

"All the guns in here are categorized," Sanders said, showing a display of the entire chamber. "Just from here, I see 'Cicero,' 'Pittsburgh,' 'Detroit.'"

Lavoie bit at her nail, narrowing her eyes at the monitor. "How odd," she said.

"What?" Koven glanced at her from his periphery. "This must be their storage facility, where they keep supplies before and after every sale. We hit the jackpot, Miriam!"

"Right, but..." she hesitated. "No, of course. That would make sense."

"This is great," Koven said. "All that's left is to find Noa."

- Niagara-on-the-Lake. Saturday, March 1 -

"Wow, how fancy!" Elli called out in a sing-song voice, entering through the doors of their new office building. "A TV and everything! Whose idea was that?"

From behind the LCD display, Noa smiled sheepishly. "It's not set up yet, but I figured it might help with, like, live business news and stuff."

Joining Nick on a freshly unwrapped couch, Mike exhaled a dramatic, heaving sigh. "Yeah, we did a lot while you girls were out. Where's Luce?"

Elli rolled her eyes, retrieving a Styrofoam box from her bag. "Not to worry sugar, I've got your order of blintzes right here. Lucy forgot something at the Luna, a scarf – I think? She told me to head here while she stopped by to pick it up."

"Probably doesn't want to help unpack either," Nick said.

"Oh, hush." Elli handed the container to Mike, placing her hands on her hips. "It isn't even that much, all the proper storage stayed underground. This is mostly paperwork."

"Yeah, try saying that while lifting a couch," Nick said with a sneer.

Hoping to cease the beginnings of a petty squabble, Noa finished hooking up the TV and flipped it on.

"Hey, way to go, kiddo!" Mike said, mouth full of crepes. "See if any games are on."

Elli flicked him playfully upside the head. "I thought we were using it for news? Turn it to local news or CNN, hon'."

Noa changed the channel to the regional news station.

"*—fficers aren't disclosing any more information so far, but we do know that the alleged kingpin of this criminal syndicate has been arrested and taken into custody.*"

A stylish news anchor stood in front of the Polar Parlor, holding a microphone in one gloved hand and gesturing to the Parlor with the other.

"*The ice cream shop behind me, an apparent front for their illegal operations, has been temporarily possessed by the state. The war on crime in New York is a continuous battle and—*"

Nick grabbed the remote from Noa, forcefully muting the reporter and hurling the device at the floor. "What the *fuck?*"

Noa's stomach sank to his feet. A wave of panic and nausea washed over him as he continued to read the closed captions on the TV screen, sensing in his gut that somehow, he was responsible.

An eerie stillness hung over the half-furnished office as the silenced anchor handed off to another presenter behind a news desk, chyron text displaying Niagara Co.'s name.

"God," Elli said, quietly at first, pushing locks of curly hair from her face. "God, I'm such an idiot! It's not like this is the first time," she fumed, "he *always* does this to us!"

Having lost his appetite, Mike pushed away the takeout container. "Maybe it's not like that, 'El," he said. "How could he have known?"

"Oh, no," she laughed with a restrained fury, pacing the new office space. "No, no, no, no, you can bet your bottom dollar: he knew. He knew this would happen like he knew

Rossini would explode, and like he knew Rocco planned to snipe him, and God knows what else. Why can't he let us in on it *for once?*"

"I'll, um, see if I can find more information," Noa mumbled, stepping off to the side and sitting against the wall beside his backpack, afraid to be too close to the others.

They didn't hear him.

"And now they seized my Parlor!" Elli cried. "My pride and joy."

Nick had mostly composed himself, searching for articles on his phone. "Somethin's weird about these numbers, though," he said under his breath.

Mike watched the muted TV with worry. "It will be fine though, right? The Boss made it through the blast in New York, and that was nuts!"

"Unless he can pull a disappearing act, I don't think so, sugar." Elli sat on the edge of the couch, folding her arms. "This is serious. If Sebastian's out, I need to launch Deadhorse. Ready or not – I have no choice."

"The numbers are all wrong, you guys," Nick said again. "I'm sure of it now. The drugs they say they confiscated in the news don't match our inventory at all."

"What are you talking about, Nick?" Elli asked. "Who cares about some rounding error?"

"I do," he said. "I keep careful records, princess. The stuff they're sayin' isn't true."

"What does that mean?" Mike scratched at this stubble nervously. "Why would they be lying? And where is Lucy – shouldn't she be here by now? Do you think that she— no, she couldn't— could she? Oh, God, she's coming right, Elli?"

Elli put her hand on his back soothingly. "Relax, hon', it's Lucy! I'm sure she's just held up in border traffic.

Worst case, she can hold her own against some New York cops."

From a few feet away, by the farthest wall, undercover agent Noa Sinclair could hear their conversation loud and clear. The blood from his head and hands had abandoned its post and he sat frozen to his laptop keyboard.

He knew why the numbers in the news didn't match Nick's records. He knew why Lucy hadn't shown up yet. He knew because his boss informed him.

```
[NS | 9:20 PM] anyway
[NS | 9:21 PM] that was all
[NS | 9:21 PM] have a good night
[AK | 8:00 AM] Noa — are you safe? Please
respond ASAP.
[AK | 8:01 AM] We have apprehended the NL-
9009 woman.
[AK | 8:01 AM] We have apprehended the
boss.
```

- Unknown location. Sunday morning, March 2 -

"We're missing a key piece of the puzzle. It's very frustrating."

"Check; watch your corners."

A frustrated slide of a plastic pawn. "There are too many inconsistencies."

"I agree."

"Nové clearly knew we were coming but didn't know *we* were coming. He cleared the place with the knowledge of a leak but didn't know Noa's true identity."

"Very odd. Your king is open to my queen's bishop."

"Damn it, Miriam. Who brings a chessboard on a mission? It isn't even a Friday," Koven groaned, moving the king.

"It helps me focus," she said matter-of-factly. "Besides, we missed our weekly game." She picked up a knight, balancing it on the tip of her finger. "Something else has been bothering me. The underground rooms beneath the waterfalls."

"Other than the architectural nightmare?"

"Besides that." She played the knight, focused on its position. "The labels in the firearm storage threw me off and I didn't realize why, at first. St. Lawrence, Rideau, Cicero. Those are groups of interest – mafias – from around the Great Lakes."

"Right, that makes sense, doesn't it?" Koven raised a brow. "Niagara Co.'s customers."

"No," Lavoie said firmly. "I remember now. The St. Lawrence Gang and the Rideau Family in Quebec, as well as the Cicero crew from Chicago – none of those groups are active anymore. Defunct for at least six months now."

"Hm." He moved a pawn, reflecting on the thought. "The storage could be old. Maybe they're stockpiling for a large sale?"

"Could be," she said. "But it doesn't sit right with me."

"The fact remains, we still don't know Noa's location," Koven sighed. "The NL-9000 woman is still too shaken to speak, but I'm almost certain her and Nové know where he is."

"Checkmate. Faster than usual, Alex."

"Excuse me for being slightly distracted," he huffed, reaching for a coffee mug. "Won't you ever let me win?"

Lavoie smiled coyly, packing up the board. "Another round tomorrow?"

"No, thanks," he pouted into the cup.

"You can't expect to win if you let emotion overtake your mind," Lavoie said. "This is a game of strategy and focus. Predict your opponent's thoughts; gain the upper hand. Win the match; solve the case."

Koven eyed her suspiciously. "You have an idea."

"I have an idea," she confirmed. "I was re-watching the tape of our earlier interview with Mr. Nové. He's quite calm, considering his situation. But there was one moment in particular that his façade broke, and he looked visibly shaken."

"I think I recall," Koven thought back. "When we mentioned NL-9009."

"Right. I suggest we use that to our advantage."

"I'm listening."

Lavoie finished packing up the chess pieces and leaned on her elbows atop the board.

"I propose this plan with the following three caveats. One: we are in – how would you say it? – deep shit. Our agent is missing, we have barely a sliver of evidence to detain Nové, and we still don't know squat about his methods. Two: he seems to care about the wellbeing of the NL subject. Three: CSIS has no jurisdiction over her capture or containment."

Koven sipped his coffee slowly. "What is your point regarding the last part?"

"We apprehended NL-9009 as an after-thought. Right place, right time. Obviously, we are supposed to ship her to the US government facility." Lavoie rested her chin on the back of her hand. "But what if we didn't?"

Her partner gave her a disapproving look. "I don't like where this is going, Miriam."

"We offer Nové a trade. Information in exchange for NL-9009's freedom," she said.

"And what if he reveals Noa's location and the means behind his market speculation data?"

Lavoie shrugged. "Then we set her free."

"Are you crazy?" Koven nearly knocked over his coffee mug, hitting the sides of the desk. "That's a terrible plan! She is extremely dangerous."

"Is she? It must have been, what, two years now since her escape? Perhaps she has been rehabilitated. No massacres in any of the Great Lakes Collective cities."

Koven rubbed his forehead. "I can't believe you would even consider this. Rehabilitated! More like a personal assassin for the mafia."

"Think about it, Alex," Lavoie said seriously. "Our involvement has been covered up. The public doesn't know CSIS has her in custody. If he goes for it and we get the boy's location, we'll obviously retrieve him before releasing her."

A moment of silence passed between them as Agent Koven stared at Agent Lavoie in disbelief.

"Admit it," she said. "Not a bad idea."

He hung his head in resignation. "You really believe this will work?"

"One way to find out."

Alone in the cell, Sebastian paced the small, windowless enclosure. With no watch, clock, or natural light, he had no sense of the time that had passed since he arrived... where?

He wasn't quite sure. Toronto? Ottawa? Some secret base in the middle of the Great White North? He had no way of knowing. His previously unwelcomed sense of confusion had boiled over into rage, then despair, as he tried to piece together where he went wrong.

First, the Newspaper. It had never erred before, and he had tested every aspect of its fortune-telling so carefully. From politics to pop culture to finance, it had been accurate.

Unless the paper was not at fault. Sebastian stopped mid-pace, mind racing.

Could this be a cover-up?

The Newspaper was not a seer or a prophet, he figured, but rather a glimpse of the future's news. Or rather, what the news will *report*.

He grimaced, realizing that by putting his faith into the Newspaper he had inadvertently turned it into his Achilles' heel. And now, because of that mistake, Lucy might lose her life.

Because of *his* mistake.

Sebastian's thoughts turned reluctantly to Noa. Since learning of his betrayal, the Niagara Company's boss had been subconsciously denying it, but the reality persisted despite his best efforts.

Noa betrayed them. Betrayed him. Worse yet, the treason confirmed Sebastian's suspicions. He wasn't asking questions out of curiosity, but out of an investigative drive. He didn't pass the initiation to join the team, but to get a better peek under the hood.

Upon finding out their shared connection to St. Isidore, Sebastian should have known. Many graduates go on to receive placements at investigate organizations around the world. CSIS *was* a bit obscure, but more believable than a part-time job at the Polar Parlor.

Sebastian sat on one of the chairs, placing his head in his hands.

The situation was so much worse than an unfinished plan and an annoying arrest. Somewhere in the building, he knew Lucy was alone and fearing for her fate and it was his fault.

His fault?

No, it was *Noa's* fault.

Wasn't it?

Unless...

Sebastian felt an ache manifesting in his chest as he considered the possibility that Noa acted out of revenge. Settling a grudge after more than ten years of abandonment.

His reactions seemed genuine, though, Sebastian thought desperately. The tearful reunion by the falls; the hours Noa spent treating his wounds after the blast; the careful arrangement of tropical fish in Elli's aquarium.

Was any of that geniune? No – it couldn't have been.

Sebastian sighed wearily as the cell door slid open. *Everything was a ruse.*

"Hello again," Agent Lavoie said as she entered alongside Agent Koven and took a seat. "Oh, you don't look so well, dear. Feeling okay?"

"Just peachy," he said. "How long have I been here?"

"Why do you need to know?" Koven asked, sitting down as well. "Waiting for something?"

Sebastian scoffed. "You people really are annoying. What do you want now?"

"Same as before," came the response. "Tell us the location of our agent."

"My answer is the same," Sebastian said. "Still no."

Lavoie placed a series of still shots from Agent Sanders' footage on the table in front of her, facing the captive. "Perhaps you could shed some light on the impressive gun and ammunitions collection we found in the underground tunnels beneath your winery?"

He glanced at the photos with narrowed eyes. "You cannot begin to fathom the scale of work and planning that you have ruined with your interference."

"Enlighten us," Koven said.

"How long have I been here?" Sebastian asked again. "You will find out soon enough, depending on the answer."

The agents exchanged a puzzled glance.

"Is that a threat?" Koven demanded, voice raising in volume.

"Think of it what you wish," Sebastian said tiredly. "I don't have an obligation to answer you. Honestly, I don't believe you know what to do with me."

Lavoie withheld a smile. "You really are a cheeky bastard, aren't you? We know what to do with you. We'd like to propose a trade."

He held her gaze. "A trade? What are you offering?"

"Your friend Lucy's freedom in exchange for our agent's location," she said. "And, as a gesture of goodwill, why don't you throw in your market manipulation secret sauce as well."

Sebastian shifted back in his seat, paling noticeably. "You can't be serious."

She held up one finger. "First, you tell us Noa Sinclair's location. For that, we shall safely escort NL-9009 outside this building." She held up a second finger. "Then, you tell us how you conduct your insider trading. For that, we guarantee that the US government and military will not find out her location. Otherwise, we might accidentally let it slip."

"You know what they'll do to her," he said, voice subdued, almost pleading.

"Tough choice," Lavoie said.

Sebastian bit down on sour anger, staring past the two agents with a lost focus. The life of one in exchange for the freedom of three others.

"You seem conflicted." Koven stood from the table, heading to the door with a motion to his partner. "We'll give you some time to think on it."

In the hallway just beyond the cell, Lavoie crossed her arms questioningly. "When did we decide to give him time to dwell? That wasn't part of my approach."

Koven removed his phone from his back pocket. "I know, but someone's been calling me nonstop. On a Sunday, no less." He examined the vibrating device, showing it to the other agent. "Number's withheld."

"Marketers can't call you, can they?" she asked. "Who else knows your CSIS line?"

He hit 'answer' with a shrug. "Yes? Alex Koven speaking."

"Good morning, sir," came the polite reply.

"Christ!" Koven nearly dropped his phone, whole body going rigid. "*Noa?* Is that you?"

Lavoie's jaw fell open. "*What?* Put him on speaker! Now!"

Koven fumbled with the screen, holding the phone between them. "Noa, are you safe?"

"Where the hell are you?" Lavoie shouted at the receiver.

"And are you safe?" Koven repeated.

"Yes, I'm okay," Noa said. "There's an urgent matter I need to discuss with you."

"Huh?" Koven shook his head incredulously. "Where are you, Noa?"

"That's irrelevant," he replied flatly through the speaker.

Lavoie grabbed the phone from her partner. "What the hell are you talking about? Tell us where you are this instant, young man."

There was a short pause as Noa cleared his throat on the other end of the line.

"I'd like to propose a trade," he said.

TWELVE
THE TRADE

- Niagara-on-the-Lake, Saturday afternoon, March 1 -

Noa's vision blurred as a high-pitched ringing overtook any background noise in his ears.

> *We have apprehended the NL-9009 woman.*
> *We have apprehended the boss.*

With a shaky hand, he closed the laptop and set it aside. His stomach churned. The remaining three faithful members of Niagara Co. were busy arguing a few feet away, unaware that CSIS had Lucy and Sebastian in custody.

He had no idea why his employers had chosen to infiltrate without warning. Was it his fault? The messages from Agent Koven did not sound as though he knew about Noa's change of heart about the mission.

Likewise, the people in the room appeared to be unaware of his undercover status.

He was, at the moment, Schrodinger's traitor.

Noa removed his glasses and closed his eyes in an attempt to collect his thoughts. Caught between a rock and a hard place – or a cliff and a waterfall – he had a couple options.

One: he could respond to his boss, let him know he was safe, and... and what? That he completed his mission? Technically not, since the insider trading was still beyond his understanding, but he could just return to Toronto and pick up a new case. Back to normal.

Right? It is *an option,* he mused to himself. He successfully stayed undercover and single-handedly led to the arrest of a wanted criminal and runaway military fugitive. He might even get promoted.

Lucy's government file flashed behind his eyes. And Sebastian... Guilt gnawed at Noa's insides. He couldn't simply abandon them, criminals or not.

Option two: confess to Niagara Co.

Noa glanced up at the blurry figures of his likely soon-to-be-ex-teammates. He could, theoretically, just stand up and come clean about everything.

He thought through that possibility. They might kill him; they might not believe him; or they might be sympathetic to his situation and work together to find a solution.

On the bright side, he reasoned, two of the three intimidating Niagara Co. members weren't around. Then he frowned shamefully at the thought. The situation was undoubtedly his fault.

Option three: run. He could sneak out, break contact with both the Niagara Co. and CSIS and disappear into obscurity without a trace.

But where would he go?

Other than his job and the people he met over the last several weeks, Noa was alone. St. Isidore didn't accept returns. No friends or family. The closest to family he had was... Sebastian.

He wrapped his arms around his knees. If there was a chance, just the slimmest hope of fixing this mess, he would take it.

"I need to start making some calls," Elli said, breaking through his thoughts. "Noa, hon', can you— oh, love. What's wrong?" She crouched down beside him. "You worried about Bassie?"

"Hey, it'll be ok, kiddo," Mike said unconvincingly, noticing his presence again. "The Boss will find a way out. If I had a dollar for every time one of us got into trouble, I'd have, like, twenty-seven dollars!"

Noa stood hesitantly, opting to keep his glasses off. *Now or never.* "There's something I need to tell you guys."

When the three others turned to him inquisitively, Noa focused all his energy on keeping his voice from shaking. He took a deep breath.

"I know where Sebastian is."

Mike blinked. "Well, yeah. We all do. The state troopers got to him."

"No," Noa swallowed, shifting on his feet uncomfortably. "They didn't. That must have been a cover up, I'm guessing. NYSP and narcotics had nothing to do with the raid. Both Sebastian and Lucy probably aren't even in the States."

"I knew it!" Nick said triumphantly. "My record-keeping is pristine— eh, wait. What are you sayin', exactly?"

Elli stood back up, retreating to the armrest of the couch. "How do you know this, sugar?" she asked worriedly. "Why would Luce and Bassie be together? And where?"

"They're, um, probably here in Canada," Noa said quietly. "Though I'm not certain."

A collection of confused responses bounced off the trio.

"What would Canadian cops want with 'em?" Nick asked.

"And why Lucy?" Mike added anxiously.

Noa fidgeted with the temples of the glasses. "They're not cops, exactly. More like the Canadian version of the CIA. They've been after Sebastian for insider trading. As for Lucy... I'm not sure how or why they captured her."

Elli listened with concern. "Canadian CIA? How can you be sure?"

Now or never, he repeated again. *Do or die. Potentially literally.* "Because I, um. I work for them."

Silence.

Unable to stand the absence of both sight and sound, Noa put his glasses back on, bracing himself for the worst.

The faces of the Niagara Co. were blank.

Mike broke the stillness with a hearty chuckle. "Good one, kiddo! Almost fooled me for a sec, talkin' all serious."

Startled at the sudden noise, Noa nearly jumped. "No, I'm not joking. I wish I were." He grabbed his laptop, then looked to Elli. "I'm not an exchange student from abroad and I'm not in high school. I work for the Canadian Security Intelligence Service. I came here to investigate the Niagara Company to find the methods behind your market manipulation."

He routed through a VPN and displayed his investigative credentials on the screen, handing the computer to Elli.

Elli took it carefully, holding the laptop as though it might explode. *"Special Agent Noa Sinclair,"* she read aloud clinically. *"Cybercrime and Financial Crime Transnational Taskforce."*

"So, you... This whole time, you've been spyin' on us?" Mike asked in disbelief.

"Not all of you, not exactly," Noa said quickly. "My focus was the insider trading. I reported back on random stuff here and there, but I swear this raid was beyond me! They didn't tell me they were coming."

No one responded. Elli stared at the words on the computer screen, the usual glimmer in her sea-green eyes fading into a dark, distant void. Mike wore a baffled expression, while Nick's face contorted with confusion and a sprinkling of anger.

"Wait, but, you should know," Noa added in a ramble, "I decided to stop reporting back! I came to value the team more than my job and didn't want you guys to get in trouble. And I found out Sebastian was— is—" his breath hitched a little, "Well. I guess I was too late. He's gone! It's all my fault."

Standing from the couch abruptly, Nick left the room with a word.

Noa desperately turned to the two others. "I'm so sorry," he said with a slight tremble. "I can't begin to apologize. I was planning on quitting the case, really, I was! I don't know why they came so suddenly! And they're probably looking for me."

Elli placed the laptop down on the floor. "How much do they know?"

Noa faltered. He had never heard her voice drop to such a pitch before. "Um, not much. I couldn't find any evidence about the insider trading. Just the two locations, and some basic descriptions. My boss harbored suspicions about Lucy's identity – he must've acted on that."

"So, they know about Lucy," Mike said under his breath. "Not good."

"I never meant for that to happen," Noa asserted. "I know about her past; I read her file. I would never want her to be captured. I didn't want any of this to happen, please believe me!" He begged, "Please don't kill me."

Elli drew in a frustrated breath, crossing her arms. "You have no idea what you've done, letting him get captured," she said. "So many years of planning. So much time and effort."

Noa tried to read her expression. "What do you—"

"We aren't going to kill you," she said.

"You're not?" he asked uncertainly.

"Sebastian means the world to us. We would take a bullet for him." Elli paused, letting the words hang in the air. "But I can see how much he means to you, too." She gazed down at the laptop. "That story your told me about your 'friend from overseas' that had to choose between his job and his loved ones. That was you, wasn't it?"

Noa nodded, overwhelmed with relief in Elli's presence.

"I don't think the Boss would forgive us if we killed ya," Mike added. "'Sides, if you work for those Canadian guys, maybe you can get us in there to set them free?"

"I'll do whatever I can!" Noa couldn't believe their kindness. On the verge of tears, he picked the laptop back up. "I can try to track them down; negotiate with them."

"Good. But don't reckon this a forgiveness," Elli said, eyes narrowing. "That'll be Bassie's decision."

"Right—"

"Are you *fucking* kidding me?" A fist slammed against the wall with a bang, drawing their attention to Nick in the office doorway.

Noa reeled at the outburst, taking an involuntary step backwards and tripping on a stack of cardboard boxes. He managed to prevent the computer from hitting the floor as he fell, landing next to a toppled box of documents.

"He's a fucking *spy* and you won't give him so much as a slap on the goddamn wrist?" Nick demanded, advancing into the room.

"Chill out, Nick," Elli said firmly. "We need his help to get them back. He could have chosen to stay quiet, and we'd be in an even bigger mess."

Nick broke into a sarcastic laugh. "Wow! This is favoritism if I ever did see it! How the hell do you know he'll help? Or that he even can?"

Processing the shock of the impact, Noa glanced at the box that fell over in front of him. Among the folders that slid onto the floor, oddly, so too did the faded pages of a newspaper.

- Unknown location. Sunday morning, March 2 -

"I'd like to propose a trade," Noa said.

Agent Koven stared at his cellphone in bewilderment. "A *trade*?"

The young voice on the other end didn't waver. "Yes, sir. I have something I would like to exchange for your two captives."

Agent Lavoie, still holding her partner's phone, raised her voice. "You must be joking. You want us to release these criminals? Are you nuts?"

"I assure you, it will be worth your while," he replied.

"*Pardon?*" Lavoie was struck with rage. "Listen here, you little brat. We risked our lives and our reputations to cross the border and rescue you. Are you saying that you were never in any danger? That you *purposely* tried to throw Alex off the fugitive's tail with those messages?"

"Ah." A brief pause on the other end preceded a hum of

realization. "That's why you came. Damn. You already knew it was her and just sat on the information."

Koven took his phone back from a seething Agent Lavoie. "Noa, is this— are you betraying us?"

They heard a dejected sigh through the speaker.

"Please believe me, sir. I didn't mean for this to happen! But with all due respect, you ruined everything by raiding them."

Lavoie's eyes bulged, "*We* ruined—"

"Anyway, that doesn't matter now," Noa continued. "Here is my proposed trade: Sebastian Nové and NL-9009 in exchange for the means by which the Niagara Co. conducts its insider trading."

"*Bon*, so, you finally completed your mission?" she scoffed. "You really think we would agree to this exchange – that we wouldn't just figure it out ourselves?"

"Respectfully, ma'am, you wouldn't," Noa said flatly. "You will see what I mean when I show you. But if you don't believe me, I can prove it. I have inside knowledge that this afternoon, AT&T will announce an acquisition of DirecTV. It's a $49 billion deal."

Koven mentally noted the information but looked at the phone in disappointment. "You do understand that your actions will result in your termination from CSIS and likely deportation from Canada, right Noa? Are you sure you want to do this?"

"Yes, I do," Noa answered quickly. "If you choose to accept my proposal, meet me on Robinson Island, tomorrow morning, 7:50 AM. Bring the captives."

There was a beep, followed by a dial tone.

"He hung up," Koven said slowly.

"Pardon my French but *what the fuck?*" Lavoie

demanded rhetorically. "Was that really Noa Sinclair? Our little Red?"

"Sounds like he defected to the other side," Koven said with a frown. "Why would he do this? After all the effort he spent getting this job and tracking them down?"

Lavoie crossed her arms. "I wonder. The photo, Alex. Both Nové and Red attended the same school – could they know each other? Bit of an age difference, but that's quite a connection."

"You're right," he said. "An incredible coincidence, actually. What are the odds?"

"About as high as the boy predicting an acquisition that hasn't happened," she replied, skimming her own smartphone for news articles. "What do you think? Should we just issue an international warrant for his arrest?"

Koven furrowed his brows, bringing a hand to his temples. "I don't know, Miriam. If Noa teamed up with the mafia, whether or not we keep Nové detained, he might have solid connections now. Do we want to make an enemy of him? He knows our system inside out."

"How embarrassing," she said. "Alright. Let's wait and see if his inside scoop is legitimate. If it is, may as well hear him out. But he needs a good slap upside the head."

Koven shrugged. "You were planning on releasing NL-9009 in exchange for information yourself. You two aren't so different."

"Do *you* want a slap upside the head?" Lavoie spun on her heel and left the hall.

The other agent followed with a light chuckle, setting the alerts on his phone to notify him about any breaking business news.

Even without a watch or a clock, Sebastian knew that many hours had passed since the two Canadian agents visited him that morning. He waited and waited and waited, but no one had returned to ask about his decision.

Part of him felt relief, as he hadn't been able to reach one.

But the other part was overwhelmed with worry. What was taking so long?

From his uncomfortable position on the rigid cot, his gaze drifted to the door. Faint footsteps approached his cell. He stood quietly, moving to the side of the door and awaiting the visitor.

A rectangular sliding hatch in the middle slid open and a tray of food edged inside. From the light in the hallway, Sebastian could see the agent's badge read 'Lee, Thomas'.

He grabbed the tray in a swift motion and tugged it inwards, startling the man on the other side of the cell. Discarding the food, Sebastian grabbed the agent's wrist and pulled it through the hatch, slamming him against the door in the process.

"Ow!" Agent Lee's face impacted with the hard surface. "Hey! Let go!"

Notwithstanding the sleep deprivation and lack of any real sustenance, Sebastian held on with surprising strength. "Where are the other two?"

"Hey man, I'm not your enemy," Lee said nervously, trying to pull free unsuccessfully. "I don't know anything."

Sebastian held his grip, bending the agent's limb at an uncomfortable angle. "That is unfortunate. I don't want to hurt you, but I can do considerable damage to your arm if you don't answer truthfully."

Lee gave a nervous laugh, struggling against the cold of the door. "What was the question again?"

"Where are the other two agents – the ones that spoke to me before? Lavoie and K-something," he said.

"Oh, Alex and Miriam? They're still here," Lee replied genuinely. "Running around like headless chickens about some trade."

"Yes, we discussed a trade," Sebastian said. "They were going to return for my decision later this morning."

"Oh, yeah, no. The decision's been made already," Lee clarified.

"What?" Sebastian's grip loosened momentarily, giving the agent a chance to free his arm from the hatch. "How have they made a decision? What changed?"

Lee rubbed his shoulder with a wince. "Look, man, I don't know the details. I shouldn't be telling you anything. One moment Alex is shouting about an AT&T merger, and the next we're planning a trip somewhere."

As realization dawned on him, Sebastian leaned against the wall with a quiet thud.

No, he thought, *anything but that.*

- Niagara-on-the-Lake. Saturday afternoon, March 1 -

Tuning out Nick's ranting, Noa watched the newspaper slide out of a folder and onto the hardwood before him. He thought it strange that among the most urgent items chosen for a last-minute move, a newspaper would make the cut.

"I don't think you two fully grasp the situation," Nick went on, "or you wouldn't be this fuckin' calm. This kid ruined *everything*."

"Yelling about it won't amount to a hill of beans," Elli countered. "Just let me concentrate! Not all is lost – we'll get them back somehow. And we still have Deadhorse."

Nick clenched his fists. "That's not the *point*. Don't you

see? He destroyed us. The base is gone. If they found any of the access doors, the underground might be gone. Deadhorse'll only launch half-finished! Your ice cream parlor's gone, princess!"

Her lip quivered slightly. "...I know that."

"But that's not all, oh no," Nick continued, pacing back and forth. "We lost Seb and Lucy to the fuckin' Canadian feds! And for what? For taking in this stupid kid!"

Mike raised his hands in a diplomatic gesture. "Mistakes happen, Nick. We all screw up. He can help us rescue them and make amends."

"Amends? Fuckin' *make amends,* man?" With a joyless laugh, Nick reached into his jacket. "Amends! The kid singlehandedly screwed us over." In a brisk move, he whipped out a pistol and aimed it squarely at Noa's head. "Amends my ass."

"Jesus Christ, Nick—" Elli leapt up from the couch in an instant, "Put that away!"

Nick narrowed his eyes on the redhead, unflinching. "No way, babe. He should suffer like my Angie suffered. Why does he get special treatment – 'cause you like him? 'Cause the Boss does? Compared to this kid's betrayal, Angie barely made a dent!"

Noa snapped back to reality to find himself staring down the barrel of a gun. Panic engulfed him, recalling Nick's promise to hurl traitors into the Hell's Half Acre.

Without hesitation, Elli stepped over the boxes of toppled documents and planted herself between them, shielding Noa with her body. "Put it away," she said in a warning tone.

Nick scoffed. "Or what?"

"You're barking up the wrong tree, Nicky." Elli stared

him down. "You think I can't handle boys like you? I will break your fucking arm."

Mike circled around them awkwardly. "Please, guys, no violence! We already lost two people."

"Give me one good reason," Nick said, holding Elli's stare. "One reason why I shouldn't kill him."

"You're of mafia blood, Nicky – you respect chain of command, right? It's simply not your call," she said sternly. "He ultimately betrayed Bassie, and Bassie's the Boss. He makes the decision."

Nick pondered the thought, unconvinced.

With a hesitant crinkle of paper, Noa peeked out from behind Elli's legs. "What if I had a way to get Sebastian and Lucy back?"

Elli glanced behind her. "You do?"

Noa nodded timidly, glancing up at Nick with caution.

"..." He lowered the gun but kept his stance. "I'm listening. You got 30 seconds."

Noa held up the Old York Tribune. "This is the key!"

Nick eyed the paper. "You better be joking, kid. Twenty-five seconds."

"No, no, look here," Noa said desperately, pointing to the header. "This must be how Sebastian predicts everything!" He was so fired up now that the words tumbled out in a flurry. "It makes sense; this is how he knew about the blast and about all the market movements and even about his arrest! This is amazing, I can't believe it—"

"Slow down!" Mike interrupted. "What are you saying?"

Noa paused for a breath. "The *date!*"

The trio leaned in for a better view of the front page.

"Sunday, March 2nd," Elli read out. "But today's the first."

"So, what?" Nick said, "A newspaper with a typo?"

"*Thinkaboutit!*" Noa could hardly contain himself. "Why would Sebastian store it in his office? Why would he get you to bring it here, Mike? Why would he hide something like this – a *regular regional newspaper?*" He pointed to the day's news. "It writes about events that haven't happened yet! Look, these hockey games, right? *Tonight's* results: right there!"

Elli blinked. "You can't be serious, sugar. A newspaper from the future? Bassie is Marty McFly?"

Noa clutched the paper urgently. "Elli, you of all people must have wondered how he did it! Listen, I wracked my brain for weeks, and there is no way anyone can get inside information on such a massive scale – no way!"

Her brows knitted together. "He never did tell me how he got the info."

"Is this the best you got, kid?" Nick asked bitterly. "Magic gazette?"

"Okay, well, it's easy to verify!" Noa stood hastily, checking his watch. "It's just past 1:00 PM now, but this sports section has the NHL results for all of Saturday's matches. All we have to do is turn on some sports network and check to see if it's right about the scores."

Mike took the paper from him, folding it over. "Last game in the Western conference's at 10 o'clock tonight," he said, turning the TV to a muted ESPN. "According to this thing, Flames will beat the Oilers 2-1."

"It was right about the 1 o'clock game," Elli said, watching the ticker onscreen. "Philly beat New York 4-2."

Nick scratched at his stubble with the pistol's muzzle. "Could be some sorta fluke. Or a trick the kid printed up. I won't be convinced unless all the scores are on the money."

Noa nodded eagerly. "So, wait till after ten! This must be it. I swear I won't go anywhere until you're convinced."

"Oh, you swear, do ya? Your word means nothing to me, kid."

In a smooth swing, the grip of Nick's gun collided with Noa's head. His world went dark.

- Niagara-on-the-Lake. Sunday morning, March 2 -

Noa awoke on the couch to a searing pain on the top of his head and Elli's coat covering him as a makeshift blanket.

He sat up with a wince, removing the puffy coat and pressing his hand to the developing bruise. In the room, Nick and Elli were gathered by the desk with takeout coffee cups, smartphones in hand, and Mike stood in front of the TV, holding a number of newspapers.

Noa cleared his throat. "Um. So, did it work?"

"You bet, kiddo!" Mike spun around, tossing a few different papers in his lap. "The Blackhawks wiped the floor with the Penguins, just like it said, and Tampa Bay beat Dallas, and those Habs barely won over the Leafs. All the way up to that 10PM game with the Flames."

"Down to the detail," Nick said reluctantly. "Every score."

"I knew it!" Noa grinned, looking through the papers. He picked out the Tribune. "Now it's got the Monday front page news! When did it change?"

"I couldn't believe my eyes," Elli said, mostly to herself. "At eight in the morning, the words just..." she gestured to the air vaguely with her coffee cup. "They started to move! I reckoned I was hallucinating but the boys saw it too. Now it says March 3rd."

"Yes!" Noa jumped up triumphantly, then grabbed his

head and sat back down. "This is the answer, then! It's how we can get Sebastian and Lucy back from CSIS."

Mike raised a brow. "From who's sis?"

"The Canadian CIA," Noa clarified. "The job that they, um, hired me for was figuring out how the insider trading happened. If I offer CSIS this newspaper in exchange for those two, I imagine they'd have to agree."

Elli took the newspaper from him, folding it up carefully and placing it under her arm. "It boggles my mind to think Bassie had a magical fortune-telling doohickey this whole time and never told me."

She sighed, crestfallen. "Okay, sugar. Set it up."

- Hell's Half Acre, Niagara River. Monday, March 3 -

7:45 AM. The warmth of the sun had not yet made it down to the untamed wilderness of Robinson Island. Overgrown trees trembled fiercely as a helicopter approached.

A pair of seagulls flew overhead, crying out in alarm and swerving out of the way.

Agents Koven & Lavoie stepped out onto the flattening grass, covering their ears from the roaring of the blades. Awaiting them in the field stood Noa Sinclair. In his hand, he held a Manila envelope.

Koven approached first. The best word to describe his visage would be disappointed. "Noa," he said respectfully. "I'm glad you're safe."

Of all the things his (likely ex-) boss could say, Noa did not anticipate that to be the first.

"...yeah. Thanks," he mumbled in response.

Agent Lavoie came to stand beside her partner. Though the turbulent wind from the helicopter had unraveled her usually taut up-do, she kept up her strict appearance with crossed arms and pursed lips.

"I never liked you," she said coldly. "Hate all teenagers, but you, especially."

Noa could only gaze down to his sneakers. "That's fair," he said.

"So?" she tapped a finger against her arm. "What have you got to show us? How in the world did you know about that AT&T acquisition before it happened?"

Noa checked his watch. 7:50 AM. "Did you bring them?"

With a disgruntled sigh, Agent Koven motioned to the chopper window. The door soon opened, sliding to the side with a mechanical creak.

Agent Lee led Lucy down the steps by her arm and onto the grass of the island. At least, Noa assumed the woman to be Lucy. She had shackles on her wrists and ankles, and a bag over her head.

Noa's stomach dropped at the sight. "You don't need the bag," he said. "She won't do anything. Please."

Lee looked to Koven for permission and subsequently removed the bag. Lucy's eyes fluttered open and locked onto Noa's own.

Her expression was pained. For the first time, Noa caught a glimpse of the scar around her throat, temporarily uncovered by a scarf or shawl. He tried to apologize with his eyes but was soon distracted by the door opening once more.

Practically pushed down the chopper steps by Sanders, Sebastian and the agent both stepped onto the island. For lack of a better word, Sebastian looked awful. His face was drained of color, save for the darkened circles beneath worn-out eyes. His wrists were cuffed behind his back, but even if they weren't, Noa couldn't imagine him to accomplish much in this exhausted state.

He stared off into the distant river without acknowledging the redhead's presence.

Noa wanted nothing more than to vanish from the earth. The pain he caused every person before him was almost tangible – the betrayal in the air was suffocating. He was almost tempted to jump into the Niagara rapids.

"Well, they're here," Lavoie said. "Shall we proceed?"

Noa managed a slight nod and checked his watch again. 7:55 AM. He had five minutes to explain. Carefully, he retrieved a folded newspaper from the envelope. Koven and Lavoie watched his every move as he took a few steps forward and held it out in front of them.

"What is this?" Koven asked.

Noa drew in a deep breath. "This is how the Niagara Co. has been conducting insider trading. Before you interrupt, please keep your questions to the end of my explanation because I haven't got much time."

The two agents glanced at each other in irritation but stayed quiet.

"If you'll notice," Noa continued, "the time of this issue of the Tribune is wrong. It says March 3rd, but the timestamp says 8:00 AM. That's not a typo. This news is actually that of a few minutes from now."

Koven squinted at the paper. Lavoie adjusted her glasses and did the same.

"The important part is in the business section." Noa flipped the page. The headline read *AT&T, DirecTV announce $49 billion merger*. "I had this information yesterday morning. You see where I'm going, right? Inside information about the future."

7:59 AM.

Lavoie chuckled darkly. "You can't really expect us to believe this."

"You will," said Noa. He directed their attention to the financial markets section. "Any gut feelings about how the stock market will perform today?"

"This is ridiculous," Koven said, shaking his head.

Noa watched the seconds tick by on his watch. "Please wait one moment."

8:00 AM.

The words on the pages began their metamorphosis. Lifting, rearranging, disappearing and reappearing from the paper, an entirely new set of articles replaced the Old York Tribune. The date transformed from March 3rd, 2014 into March 4th, 2014.

"What the hell...?" Lavoie muttered to herself.

Agent Koven, transfixed as well, leaned in for a better look. "How are you doing this?"

"I'm not," said Noa. "Frankly, I have no idea how it works. But I verified it, and so did you by checking on the AT&T merger for me." He pointed to the stock index, "You can see all the day's fluctuations here in advance."

"Facebook to acquire Whatsapp," Koven read aloud. "Unbelievable. This is how they did it?"

"You can wait until that news becomes public to confirm," Noa said with a nod. "It's legit."

"A magic newspaper." Lavoie took the paper in her hands. "Who could have guessed?"

"So, are we done?" Noa asked hopefully. "I upheld my end of the bargain."

She folded the paper under her arm and turned to Sebastian. "What does it feel like, Mr. Nové? Your life traded for a few flimsy pages."

Sebastian gazed up to the clouds lazily. "Bold of you to

assume you ever held my life in your hands. But I am impressed he figured it out so quickly. *Great* agent. You ought to be delighted with his work."

8:10 AM. If words could burn, Noa felt the singe on his heart.

"*Mais*, not so great, clearly," Lavoie replied. "Still, this newspaper is something else. We'll need to verify its contents and contain it."

"You have what you wanted," Noa said, his voice at a near tremble. "Let them go."

"Hm." Lavoie glanced at her partner, then shrugged. "Why? We have the evidence now. And these two are wanted criminals – we can't just let them go, can we? After all the trouble we went through."

"Really?" Noa turned to Agent Koven. "You won't honor your word?"

"I'm sorry, Noa," Koven said sadly. "Surely you must have expected this."

8:15 AM. The redhead frowned. "I did, but I was hoping otherwise. Fine. Sir, ma'am, if you don't uphold your end of our deal, I will expose all of your actions immediately."

Lavoie shot him a questioning look. "Excuse me?"

"The cover up of Niagara Co.'s raid using faked information; keeping knowledge of NL-9000 from the US government; maybe even the Tetris incident while I'm at it for good measure," said Noa. "I have a colleague ready to report it all to the press as we speak."

He watched the faces of the agents progress through the entire five stages of grief in a matter of seconds. He also noted a brief glimmer of emotion in Sebastian's eyes. Was it pride? Before Noa could tell, he looked away again.

Lavoie's grip on the newspaper tightened. "I underestimated you, Red. You are much more fit for the criminal trade than law enforcement."

"So, you'll let them go?" Noa asked again.

Koven gently tugged the paper out of her grasp. "I suppose that exposé would be on the front page if you broke the news, wouldn't it?" He flipped to the first page.

Noa noticed Sebastian's intrigue from his periphery.

8:20 AM. Lavoie peered at the breaking headline. "Project *Deadhorse*? Where have I heard that name before?"

The other agent held the paper out, concern marring his features as he skimmed the article. "Miriam, you need to see this."

8:30 AM. Monday, March 3rd, 2014. The first news coverage of *Project Deadhorse* airs on television, following anonymous tips sent with comprehensive detail by an anonymous person calling themselves Pecan Pie. CNN breaks the story with a live interview.

The Old York Tribune captures the exclusive 30 minutes in advance.

Agent Lavoie's cellphone rang out from her coat pocket and she answered it immediately.

"Miriam!" Director Colson voice shouted from the device. "Are you with Alex? Are you near a TV? Turn on the news *right now*. It's about—"

"Niagara Co.," Lavoie said softly, her eyes glued to the paper. "Yes. We know."

"What's going on?" Agent Lee watched the scene unfold with confusion. "What just happened?"

"Check the news," Sebastian told him. "Also, if you could kindly uncuff the lady and myself, I would appreciate it."

Lee hurriedly pulled up the breaking news on his cellphone, tapping on a top broadcast.

A CNN anchor sat behind the news desk. A young woman with long, dark hair and a smart suit sat across from him. Lee hit play.

"We have a breaking story this morning, in an update on Saturday's arrest of the Niagara Company's leader," the newscaster said. "I am joined by Attorney General Juliette Mercer in the studio. In a chain of events that's rocking our nation and our upstairs neighbor, what can you tell us about the Deadhorse project?"

THIRTEEN
DEADHORSE

- Lake Huron. August, 2010 -

A hot midsummer sunset settled upon the glistening clear waters of Lake Huron. Just 10 miles off the coast of Port Hope, Michigan, a glamorous yacht embossed with the title *Aurora II* sailed northeast at a leisurely pace.

Stepping out to the back deck, a recently emancipated Elise René – exclusively known now as Elli – joined the three other members of her new team topside. She removed her sunglasses and hooked them on the neckline of her top, slowly inhaling the fresh, misty air.

"So, this boat," she said, coming to stand by the ledge which overlooked the passing lake beneath them. "Just under 20 mil, right? Impulse purchase or…?"

"You've been taking a look at our books," Sebastian said passively. He was leaning on the taffrail, gazing at the waves rolling behind the ship pensively. "It's not that I dislike life ashore. But life on the water is better. Or so I've been told, by an old friend of mine."

"Hey new girl," Mike called out from the Jacuzzi on the

other end of the deck, "how good are you at geography? We've been doing this crossword forever."

Nick, lounging on a neighboring pool chair, held a newspaper folded in his hand. "Where would she have learned the capital of Comoros? Pageant school?"

"Moroni?" Elli yelled back promptly.

"Damn," Nick muttered, scribbling in the word. "It fits."

"That's m-o-r-o-n," she added loudly, "like your middle name, sugar."

"Alright, children," Sebastian said with a sigh. "Let's get along, please."

"Could I file a minor complaint to management?" Elli turned to him, leaning her elbow against the railing. "The male to female ratio of this team is very unbalanced. I think the testosterone levels are the skewing the maturity scale away from 'reasonable adult.'"

Sebastian glanced at her briefly with a slight chuckle. "Complaint noted. I'll try to remedy that. Anything else?"

"Actually, yes," she said. "I did take a look at your books. You know, since I'm assuming you hired me for my financial background."

"And? Should I be worried?" he asked, resuming his watch of the waves.

"Another one," Mike called out. "Formerly known as 'Pheasant Island,' this tiny country has been stripped clean of phosphate – mined to exhaustion by the year 2000. Any ideas?"

Elli tapped her chin. "Pheasant Island... The bird poop reserves, right? Try either Banaba or Nauru," she shouted to him.

Nick cursed quietly under his breath. "Stupid geography trivia. Who knows this crap?"

"As I was saying," Elli returned to her previous

thoughts. "Your records. You have some explaining to do, sugar. Two million dollars paid in a single instalment, two summers ago. Well-hidden too, and no detail attached except that the payment was wired from New York to Pennsylvania."

"Wonder what that could have been," he said with a coy smile.

"Uh huh." She kept her focus trained on him. "And consistent, cash donations to an auto shop in White Rock, South Carolina?"

Sebastian bowed his head slightly. "I thought those were well laundered. Either you're a very good investigator, or I'm very bad at financial fraud."

Elli gripped the taffrail with her hands momentarily. "I knew what to search for, once I realized it was you that set me free in '08." Releasing the ledge, she pivoted on her heel and embraced him tightly.

Sebastian tensed. "Elli...? What are you doing?"

"It's a hug, Bassie! I'm hugging you," she said with a laugh. "Thank you."

He relaxed somewhat, patting her back awkwardly. "My pleasure."

She let him go, taking a step back. "But why? Why me? And why now? As much as I enjoy cruising around the lakes in your mega-yacht, I want an explanation."

"You deserve one," he said earnestly, turning away from the water at last. "I followed your case in the news."

Elli blew a strand of hair from her face. "Mhm. You and a million others. So what?"

"You may not be satisfied with my answer," Sebastian said, meeting her eyes. "When I watched your trial, I was struck by your genuine pleas of innocence. And by how much you resembled my departed sister, had she grown to be your age."

She gave him an unconvinced look. "You believed I wasn't guilty because I reminded you of your dead sister?"

"No," he shook his head once. "I was fairly certain you weren't guilty because of the prosecution. July— Juliette, rather, isn't exactly known for her honest methods. When I dug deeper, into your past, family, and education, I confirmed that you were not the criminal she framed to the jury. I thought you would be the perfect person to help me with my plan."

Elli grabbed his arm, "I knew it – she's not really into girls, is she? You two were an item?" She drew in a frustrated breath. "Damn, I knew it! You can tell me; I won't be mad. You even have a cute nickname for her and everything, oh, my god."

Sebastian physically recoiled with disgust. "*Me?* And *July?*" He gently removed Elli's hand. "I assure you; I cannot imagine a fate worse than that. We were raised together. That was unfortunate enough."

Elli frowned. "Raised together? Really? She's Asian, and you're... what are you, anyway?"

"It's complicated," he said. "And not very relevant. I've lived in a lot of places."

"Okay, fine. Let's rewind a bit. What's this about a plan?"

Sebastian smiled, a mischievous gleam in his eye. "Follow me."

As the two of them headed amidship, Mike called out again.

"Hey, wait, new girl! Before you go: which country in the world has a poverty rate of zero?"

"Kind of a trick question," she said, halfway off the

deck. "Try Monaco, but only because they kick out the poor people."

"Sounds right," Sebastian said under his breath, going inside the main cabin.

Mike gave a thumbs up. "It fits! Thanks."

"You bet, sugar," Elli returned the gesture and followed Sebastian into a spacious office-like room past the bridge.

The walls were covered with pinned papers and handwritten notes, some of them linked together with string. A laptop and an assortment of documents were sprawled on a desk, most in English but a few in Italian.

Elli whistled. "Wow. Is this the part where I discover that you're a bit kooky and take off running? Or swimming to the nearest shore?"

Sebastian sat in a chair by the front of the desk. "You're free to go anytime you wish, Elli. I'm simply offering you the choice: a chance to take part in something grand. Bigger than yourself."

She glanced around the room, taking in the information on the walls. "These are other criminal syndicates around the US-Canadian border. And this one," she pointed to the papers on the table, "is that the mob you took over when you came from Venice to New York?"

"Yes." He moved a pile of documents aside, tearing a fresh page out of a large notebook. "Hear me out before you say anything."

"As long as it's not some crazed manifesto, Bassie." She sat next to him on the desk, watching with a growing intrigue.

"Not crazed, I would hope. And please stop with the nickname," he said. "I've been considering this idea for a while now – how to make a difference in my own, small way. But life and its circumstances led me down a less-than-virtuous path."

"You mean running a mafia was not your childhood dream?" Elli asked with a gasp. She watched as he sketched out a rough outline of North America on the sheet. "Remind me again why you thought I would be helpful to you?"

Sebastian continued drawing out his plan. "At first, I wasn't certain. I thought you simply had the right disposition. But after your release, I spent nearly two years searching for you, and in that time, you had built an impressive reputation for yourself. Your skills in trading, persuasion, and business management – all while on the run – were admirable."

"You flatter me! Do go on," Elli said, pressing the palm of her hand to her left cheek.

"You were accomplishing all of this as a participant in illegal underground gambling rings. Winning huge sums of money in hugely immoral ways. However," he paused, glancing up briefly. "You never spent a cent of that money unethically."

Elli swung her legs off the side of the table, considering his words. "So, you want me to act as a morally-conscious financial consultant for your mob expansion strategy?"

Sebastian shrugged. "Labels are for wine bottles, as they say. But essentially, yes."

"No one says that, Bassie."

He ignored the comment, turning the finished product of his scribbles towards her. "Here's the gist: a consolidation of criminal syndicates on a national scale. International, even. Starting with the Eastern border states and moving westward from there."

He led the pen along New York state towards the Great Lakes.

"Phase One: establish a solid reputation and grow enough capital to sustain power – I've already started with my old mob in Manhattan and Venice. Phase Two: merge with other groups, through monetary persuasion or force, and subsequently dissolve them." He circled the entire map. "Phase Three: confiscate and retain any merchandise they possessed, without selling them back into the market. Gradually deplete the trade of illegal goods."

Elli listened skeptically. "You want to build a criminal empire to abolish criminal trade? That's... surprisingly honorable. And the border?"

"Ah, therein lies the crux of the plan." Sebastian marked three lines on the map from Ontario – one to New York, one to Michigan, and one to Minnesota. "Fourteen bridges across the border, all concentrated around the Great Lakes. Control bridge traffic, control supply."

"And you already have New York," she said with a thoughtful nod. "I see. Like a Great Lakes collective. Well, this would certainly make a difference in 'some small way.'"

"Hm. Great Lakes Collective," he repeated quietly.

Elli tapped at the paper with the tip of her fingernail. "Glaring flaw in your strategy, hon'. Actually, a couple. First, your intentions will be immediately clear to any competing gangs soon enough. After you absorb and dissolve a few, word will spread – your brand will suffer. Like the Manhattan one you took over; what if that comes back to bite you?"

"Rossini? He wouldn't have the nerve," Sebastian said. "But point taken. What would you suggest?"

She hopped off the table, walking the perimeter of the cabin. "You're a business, right? It's all about the image. We shape how you're perceived. What if, when you take over or merge, you keep some shell of the old gang operating as a puppet. In reality, it'll be dissolved. But to an outsider, it will look as though they are willingly part of your growing empire."

Sebastian nodded, leaning back in the chair. "Part of the collective."

"Right! Smoke and mirrors."

"Good thinking," he said. "What's the other flaw?"

Elli stopped by the porthole, opening the window a smidge to allow the refreshing evening air inside. "I like the idea, Bassie, I really do. But it doesn't seem feasible. An operation on this scale would require insane connections. It's for a noble cause, sure, but the legality sits squarely in the no-no zone. What if there's pushback? What happens if you go public and the law disagrees with your methods?"

Sebastian folded his hands in front of him on the table. "You're right. This plan hinges on a powerful insider within the judiciary."

A warm, summer breeze drifted in through the open porthole, shuffling a few notes on the table. Other than the momentary rustling of paper, the room was silent as Elli turned to face him, her expression betraying her outrage at the implication.

"You must be joking," she said, voice faltering slightly. "Even if you reckon that I have *any* connection with her, have you forgotten that she *framed* me?"

Sebastian stood from the table. "For that reason, your involvement is crucial. Because you are Juliette's worst mistake." He walked over to a cabinet of drawers, unlocking the bottom one. "But as I mentioned before, you have a choice to make, Elli."

He retrieved a silver briefcase, placing it on the desk. She recognized it immediately.

"Your case was not the first she corrupted, nor will it be the last," Sebastian said with a solemn expression. "Unfortunately, it's the way we were brought up to succeed. But if you want, with enough time and dedication, you could take this falsified evidence, find unbought witnesses, and prove your innocence. Restore your former life. Achieve vengeance."

Elli hesitantly ran her hand along the familiar steel casing of her beloved poker set, tears threatening to materialize in the corners of her eyes. "Or?"

"Or join me and make history. Use the threat of exposing Juliette's corruption the means by which we get her onboard."

Elli hugged the silver briefcase to her chest. "You would really just give this to me and let me go? Even now that I know your name; your face; your plans?"

Sebastian sighed, running a hand through his hair. "I was hoping to convince you, but yes. Especially if it takes July down, I won't mind. I will find some other way, eventually."

She bit her lip, shifting from one foot to another. "How about a trial run?"

He extended his hand with a cordial smile. "If I can convince you in the next six months, you're in?"

She shook his hand. "Deal. Let's drink to that!"

They went back out onto the sundeck, rejoining the others. A clear night sky stretched eternally above them, dusting brilliantly shining stars far into the dark horizon.

"We'd need a cool name," Elli said. "For the plan. Some kind of code word."

Sebastian went to the bar, pouring two drinks. "What do you propose?"

She spun around on a barstool. "Something ominous, but also ambiguous. Like *Rolling Thunder* or *Barbarossa*."

"There you guys are," Mike exclaimed. "We have just one question left to finish this crossword."

"Been stuck on this one for ages," Nick grumbled. "'Located on Alaska's North Slope, this tiny town sits on the largest oil field in North America.'"

Sebastian passed her a glass. "Deadhorse," he said.

They locked eyes.

In unison, Mike and Elli blurted out, "That's it!"

FOURTEEN
DISSOLUTION

- Hell's Half Acre, Niagara River. Monday, March 3 -

8:45 AM.

Agent Lee turned off the news broadcast on his cellphone and returned it to his pocket. Agent Lavoie hung up on the Director.

"Colson's upset," she said. "I guess this explains the lack of criminal activity on the Quebec and Ontario border recently. And why those names in Sanders' exploration vlog tripped me up."

Agent Koven, still holding a tight grip on the Old York Tribune with one hand, rubbed his eyes with the other. "So, Mercer wanted the case because she was part of his plans all along?"

"Depends when she got in touch," Sebastian chimed in from the riverside. "If it was before my 'financial consultant,' as you called her, tipped off the media, then Juliette likely wanted to prosecute in either scenario."

The two agents turned to face him.

"Surprise?" he said with a shrug, then motioned to his

bound wrists with a tilt of his head. "I understand you're processing a lot, but you've made a deal with your traitorous former agent over there. And you're holding your priceless end of the bargain in your hands already."

Koven looked to the former agent in question. "Did you know about this?"

Noa was staring at his own smartphone in disbelief. "No, I... I should have realized, but no. I had no idea." He drew up a shallow breath, "If I had known, I—"

"Let me ask you something, Noa," Koven said grimly. "Whose side are you on? You've made an enemy of us, and you will not be able to work in Canada again regardless of how this plays out. Not only that, but you had made your choice believing the Niagara Co. to be a cut-and-dry mafia. And I don't hesitate to think that your deception will make them think twice about keeping you around."

Unable to respond, Noa clutched his phone in a tight grasp.

"Keep him around for *what*?" Lavoie added. "Now that this plan has been revealed, I don't suppose they could just pick up and carry on. Not to mention that everything we found since Saturday has been seized. Stored weapons, drugs; the ice cream shop and winery. That nice boat at La Salle marina."

Noa noticed Sebastian tense up a bit.

"Sounds like it's all over now," Lavoie said, straightening out her coat.

Koven folded up the Tribune, placing it inside his jacket. "What was your goal here, Noa?"

The redhead looked down uncomfortably. "I, um. I don't know. I don't know what I'm doing, but I did it. So, please, just let them go, sir."

With a sigh, Koven turned to the two agents by the

river. "Uncuff them." He smiled solemnly at Noa. "Good luck, agent. And goodbye."

As Agents Koven and Lavoie made their way back to the helicopter, Sanders unlocked Sebastian's handcuffs while Lee did the same for Lucy.

"Sorry for knocking you out before," Sanders said with a sheepish laugh. "Didn't know you were on our side all along."

Free from the binds, Sebastian massaged the indents on his wrists and considered the apology. Winding back his shoulder, he took a short step back and punched the agent squarely in the face.

"Water under the bridge," he said.

Lee backed away from Lucy hurriedly, letting her shackles fall to the ground. She went to Sebastian's side by the river, relief washing over her features.

The agents returned to the chopper, and following a final glare from Agent Lavoie, the door shut behind them. As the blades spun to life, Sebastian put an arm protectively around Lucy, turning them both away from the gusts of sudden wind.

"Are you alright?" he asked, giving her a once-over glance.

She nodded with a small smile. "Could be worse."

As the helicopter departed, so too did the noise, giving way to a pair of excited, shouting voices emerging from the trees behind Noa.

Within seconds, and with an enormous running start, Elli pounced onto Sebastian and Lucy, trapping them both in a spinning bear-hug.

"Y'all are okay!" she exclaimed. "You look like hell but you're alive!"

Sebastian returned the embrace with a chuckle and a

slight wince. "Careful; still recovering. Sorry for making you worry."

Elli broke the hug and stepped back one pace. Tears welled up in her eyes and Lucy took her cue to move aside. With a wide swing of her arm, Elli slapped Sebastian's cheek with an open palm.

Lucy covered her mouth, inching away to join an approaching Mike. He eagerly welcomed her back, draping a silky scarf around her neck and his coat over her shoulders.

Stunned, Sebastian brought a hand to his reddening cheek. "Ow. Unusual choice of greeting."

Elli punched him in the arm, then hugged him again, more delicately this time. "You idiot," she said, voice trembling. "I could've helped you! Why did you hide that stupid newspaper from me? The blast and the arrest and everything – why keep it to yourself?"

Confused by the mixed messages, Sebastian rubbed her back lightly. "I'm sorry, Elli. I didn't want to put you at risk. The future predicted in the paper couldn't be prevented anyway. Not that it matters now; it's gone."

"You could have been imprisoned! Don't you care about yourself at all?" she cried.

"You care enough for both of us," he said. "My biggest regret was not realizing I put Lucy at risk as well."

"Moron," Elli mumbled into his shirt. "Ain't got the good sense God gave a rock. I missed you."

Sebastian smiled fondly. "I missed you too. And I missed *you*, Mike."

The words flew over Mike's head, as he was pre-occupied inspecting Lucy for injuries.

"Are you okay, Luce? Did they hurt you? Did they

threaten you? Did they *threaten* to hurt you?" Mike grasped her hand. "Did you eat properly? Did you sleep?"

Lucy leaned forward, pressing their foreheads together. "I am fine. Really."

"Oh, it must've been awful; I should've been there with you!" Mike lamented.

She patted the back of his hand. "Not so bad. Nice facilities."

Elli pulled her back in for another hug. "Thank the lord they didn't extradite you!"

"Yes," Lucy agreed. "I thought they might."

Mike went over to Sebastian, shaking his hand with a grin. "I'm glad you're all good too, Boss! But you do seem a bit sleep deprived. Not to say you look bad! Just... less than great."

"Thanks Mike," he replied. "I will admit I could use some rest."

"Then let's skedaddle," Elli said cheerfully, arm around Lucy. "Nicky's waiting with the car."

Throughout the commotion and reunions by the riverside, Noa stayed quiet, awkwardly shifting back and forth on his feet. He was relieved that the plan worked perfectly, and simultaneously taken aback by the revelation that he had overlooked a much bigger strategy entirely.

Unsure what they would do with him now, he kept his gaze lowered, studying the blades of grass beneath his shoes.

"Let's hurry," Mike said, leading the group away from the river and towards the trees. "You guys must be starving too!"

Sebastian followed, with Elli and Lucy arm-in-arm close behind.

"Well, don't just stand there," Elli said as they passed by

Noa. "You did your part, hon'. Least we can do is return you to the mainland."

Wordlessly, Noa followed after them, keeping some distance.

Mike stopped before a flattened patch of dirt that lay in the center of three large trees, kneeling down to uncover a hidden metallic hatch. Still unlocked from the morning's usage, he popped it up and held it open for Lucy and Elli to descend first.

"Never thought we'd need the Robinson exit," Sebastian said, descending after them. "Nice to see it put to use."

"It was Noa's idea," Mike said as the redhead approached. "Good job, kiddo. Your plan went off without a hitch."

Noa mumbled a thank you, waiting for Mike to go down the exit before him. He then shut the access hatch, locking it in the same manner as he unlocked it earlier that morning.

The group made their way through the underground tunnel and emerged through another locked door into a familiar rounded chamber encircled by labeled entrances.

"Which storage chambers have been compromised?" Sebastian asked.

"Just Canada and America," Mike said. "Those were the flimsiest locks, after all. And I guess they didn't want to bomb the place."

"Doesn't mean this stuff is safe though," Elli interjected. "And neither are we, so no stalling. They might come back anytime."

She took the lead, unlocking a series of mechanical bolts and digital passcodes on the door labeled 'Goat.' Once open, she motioned for the others to proceed. After another few minutes in the underground tunnel, Elli stopped at a ladder and climbed up, unfastening another locked hatch on the ceiling.

One by one, the five of them climbed out in an isolated section of woods, obscured by the Cave of Winds on Goat Island. Hurrying to avoid drawing any attention from the early-arriving tourists, Elli navigated to Nick's awaiting car, in which they promptly crossed the 1st Street bridge from Goat Island onto the New York mainland.

9:30 AM. The Niagara Co. was reunited.

- Niagara-on-the-Lake. Monday afternoon, March 3 -

It was a tense drive back for Noa, sandwiched between Mike and Elli in the back seat of Nick's car.

During the short drive to the office on the lake, Sebastian recounted the events from last winter and how he came into possession of the Old York Tribune. He told them about the madman in the mansion, the fire, all the experiments he ran to test the paper's accuracy.

Upon arriving at the new office, their conversations fizzled out. Standing outside the front entrance, Elli twirled a lock of hair uneasily, curling it around her finger.

"So, what now? I reckon the Polar Parlor is gone for good?"

Sebastian glanced up at the two-story building, seeing it personally for the first time. "Now, the Niagara Co. is going to undergo some restructuring. I'd been preparing a Plan B for situations such as this one. Give me a few hours," he said, hand on the doorhandle. "I'll speak with each of you then."

On the second floor of the new office space, Sebastian leaned against the windowsill with a worn-out sigh. Half empty, most of the room remained unassembled. Just a rounded table with a couple seats stood in the center, with stacks of boxes and cabinets that he had mandated for the move crowding the corners.

He closed his eyes for a temporary reprieve. "What a mess."

From the moment he read the article about his arrest, he knew there was a chance for his plans to unravel. He just hadn't realized how bad of a reality awaited him. A betrayal from within. A cover-up that targeted the newspaper's weakness. An international agency involved for months without his knowledge.

And now, because of his carelessness, the Deadhorse Plan could only be carried out to a limited extent. Despite the consolidation of the Great Lakes region and along the US-Canadian border, his vision extended much farther. But the publicization was Juliette Mercer's one condition – to ensure her name was clear in case his fate was sealed.

Like the Tribune's.

He doubted it would ever see the light of day again. Confined to some containment chamber or testing facility.

It could have been worse than this, he thought with a frown. He could have lost Lucy, or the rest of his team.

Sebastian opened his eyes. His team. The team that relied on him for his leadership. One last time...

After washing up and changing out of his captivity clothes with a spare set packed away in a cabinet, and some time spent making calls and rummaging through boxes trying to locate his old safe files, Sebastian called in his team.

Just the original four, naturally.

Nick came in first, followed by Mike and Lucy together, and Elli trailing in last. The girls took the two assembled chairs, while the two others stayed standing.

"Are we just going let him leave, chief?" Nick asked apprehensively.

Sebastian blinked. "Pardon?"

"The kid," he clarified. "Should I have tied him up or somethin'?"

Sebastian shook his head tiredly. "Noa won't leave. I'll deal with him later."

"How can you be so sure?" Nick demanded. "He'll run!"

"Don't worry about him," Sebastian reiterated, voice calm. "I need to speak with the four of you first. This is more important."

Mike watched him nervously. "What's up, Boss? You've got a way to fix things, right? Like you always do?"

A pang of guilt blended with the weight of exhaustion already sitting on Sebastian's shoulders. "Unfortunately, things aren't quite fixable this time. Plan B is less solution and more... reinvention."

He glanced around the room, welcomed by an unexpected silence. Usually, someone would chime in or interrupt. Not this time. The forlorn and concerned expressions on his teammates' – no, on his friends' – faces were harrowing.

Sebastian took in a deep breath, laying out a series of envelopes on the table. "To put it simply," he said, "I am dissolving the Niagara Co. And it is time for us to go our separate ways."

With a hesitant smile, Elli pressed her hands together in her lap. "Bassie, are you breaking up with us?"

"That's a regrettable way of putting it, but I suppose,"

he said, raking a hand through his hair. "With the fallout of Deadhorse, it isn't safe to be associated with me anymore. I have nothing left to offer you – and even if I did, it wouldn't be worth the risk. Before you worry, I have several options available for each of you—"

"Wait, wait, pause!" Mike took a step forward. "Are you kiddin'? We're not leaving you! We're a team!"

"Second that," Nick added, Elli and Lucy nodding along.

"We can survive," Mike said. "Just because DH went belly-up and our stuff is gone, doesn't mean we can't start over! You're not getting rid of us."

Sebastian smiled solemnly. "I'm touched; thank you. But I've made my decision."

"We don't get a vote?" Elli asked, crossing her arms. "You can't just order us to leave!"

"Please," he said earnestly. "Just hear me out. This does not mean I won't see you again. In due time, I will reconnect with all of you. But for now, it isn't safe. Regardless of what you say, I will disappear from the country tomorrow."

"You can't be serious," Mike said. "Where will you go? Where will *we* go?"

"Don't worry," Sebastian replied, pushing the envelopes forward. "I'm getting to that."

Time trickled by slowly. A growing breeze whisked ripples over the lake like folds on a worn and wrinkled sweater. Minutes turned into hours and the rays of the noontime sun disappeared behind treetops and buildings.

Curiously, pedestrians would glance at the lone figure sitting on the curb outside a seemingly unused retail office.

An older woman stopped mid-stride to smile comfortingly at the teenager and held out a ten-dollar bill.

"Here, darling. Get yourself something to eat," she said.

Startled out of his thoughts, Noa peered up at the woman. "Sorry?"

"You look famished, love." She placed the purple bill in front of him. "I suggest you bring a cup or something next time. Makes it easier for people to give donations."

Noa took the cash apprehensively. "Um, I'm not homeless." The woman had already walked away though, so he pocketed the money.

The early March chill was creeping through his hoodie, but he had gotten too restless waiting inside and spent the past couple hours waiting on the sidewalk. Fully realizing that he could leave, an unknown force compelled him to stay.

Sebastian said he would speak to *each of them*. That meant Noa too, right?

He briefly considered creeping upstairs to eavesdrop but decided against it after recalling his previous attempt in the underground office. He kicked a pebble with his foot, sighing in frustration.

Why couldn't he just leave, for God's sake? He had enough money to get out of Niagara, he could just leave and go... where?

Right. That was the reason.

Noa pressed his knees to his chest, resting his head on them. He sat on the street for longer than he could remember, with no inkling of what to expect. Finally, startled by the sound of the door swinging open, he stood.

Elli stepped out of the building, alone. She had faded streaks of mascara staining her cheeks.

"Hey, sugar," she said softly. "You're still here. Good. Bassie wants to see you."

Noa's heart rate picked up its pace. "He does?"

"Relax, he won't kill ya or anything," she said with a fading smile. "But first, I wanted to talk to you."

Noa gave an uncertain nod.

"I consider this whole predicament to be my fault." Elli took a step toward the curb, watching the cars pass by. "If I hadn't asked Bassie to give you a job, we wouldn't be in this mess."

"No, no! Please don't blame yourself," Noa protested. "I'd have found another way in!"

Elli wiped some dried makeup from her cheek. "It's alright. What's passed is past."

"I really am sorry," Noa lowered his head.

With another short step, Elli pulled him in for a hug. "I know."

Noa returned the embrace wordlessly, face buried in her peach and vanilla-scented curls.

She put her hand on the back of his head. "You're not a bad person, Noa. In another life, I reckon all of us could have been a team. I can't speak for the others, but I forgive you."

Tears stung at the corners of his eyes. "You do?"

Gently, and much to Noa's reluctance, Elli broke the hug. "I do. And I wanted to give you a proper goodbye and wish you only the best. Hopefully one day we'll meet again."

His stomach sank at the words. "You're leaving?"

As if on cue, an approaching cab pulled up to the side of the curb.

Elli put her hand on Noa's cheek. "Go upstairs. If

Bassie thinks you ran away, things will be much worse for you."

"But—"

"Goodbye, sugar." The driver of the cab got out of the car and held the door open for Elli. She waved as the vehicle departed, leaving him alone on the curb again.

Mustering up the courage to go inside and compelling himself not to cry, Noa turned to the building. Before he had a chance to enter, though, he spun around at the sound of another vehicle approaching.

A cherry red convertible stopped before the building. Its driver stepped out, removing her sunglasses and taking in the surroundings. Noa recognized her almost immediately from the news.

"...Attorney Mercer?"

She zeroed in on him with a sharp focus. "Where is Elise? Er, Elli. Did she leave already?"

"Um, yes," he said, brows knitting in confusion. "She just left. How do you know Elli?"

"*Tsk*," she bit at her thumbnail, opening the car door again. "Damn. Alright, forget I was here."

Noa approached her vehicle. "You were part of their project, weren't you? Deadhorse?"

She hesitated, studying his features for a moment. "Wow," she said with a sudden laugh. "*November?*"

He drew in a sharp breath. "What? But how—"

"Jesus Christ," Juliette muttered under her breath, putting her sunglasses back on. "Who were you with, CSIS? To think they would stoop so low. Listen, I need to run. But call me," she shoved a business card into his hands. "We should talk."

Dumbfounded, Noa stared down at the card as the red

convertible sped away from the curb. He put the card in his pocket with the ten-dollar bill from earlier.

Channeling any remaining energy, Noa went inside at last.

Afraid to lose his motivation, he hurried up the stairs. He paused at the closed door, his fingers hovering nervously over the doorknob.

He could still leave. Turn around and walk out the exit—

"Come in."

Too late.

Exhaling nervously, he opened the door. He made his way past the chairs, coming to stand by the table. Sebastian stayed at the window, his back to Noa.

"How did you know I was there?" the redhead asked quietly.

"I can hear your heart pounding from across the room. Please calm down – I'm not going to hurt you," Sebastian replied, watching the dusk settle over the town.

Noa put a palm reflexively over his chest. "Oh."

"Nick told me what happened on Saturday," Sebastian added. "I apologize for that. If it makes you feel any better, the gun was empty."

"Oh," Noa said again.

Sebastian turned to face him. He held an envelope in his hand, which he placed atop the barren table.

"I must admit, Noa," he said, "you blindsided me. Then again, I had never taken on a challenger with the same upbringing. I have just one question: who do you regret betraying more?"

"You, of course!" Noa exclaimed, shocked at the question. "I mean, I definitely regret putting Agent Koven through the wringer, but it had to be done."

"Oh?" Sebastian arched a brow, leaning against the windowsill. "Well, life is one large regret and then we die. Tell me, how did you plan to balance an undercover job at CSIS and moonlighting here? Wait long enough for the storm to break and wash away your mistakes?"

Noa clenched his sweater sleeves in his fists. "I— I don't know. I had a clear goal at the start: to take you down. Things got complicated when I got to know you guys, and when I found out who *you* were, I wanted to stop the whole investigation!"

"But you didn't stop it."

"I tried," Noa said, mouth going dry. "That's, um. Well, I made a mistake. I tried throwing CSIS off Lucy's track, but they thought I was taken hostage. That's why they infiltrated suddenly – without warning me!"

"Hm." Sebastian scoffed with slight amusement. "So, you even blindsided yourself."

Noa looked down. "If not for that, I would have told you everything. I just needed time to prepare an explanation. And I swear, if I had known about your horse plan, I would never have pursued this investigation in the first place."

A brief silence passed between them.

Sebastian slid the envelope across the table, keeping his distance.

Noa eyed it warily. "What's this?"

"Consider it a severance package from Niagara Co.," he replied. "You were my employee for a short while, after all."

"I don't understand. You're giving me money? Why?"

"Not only money. Inside, you'll find tickets and the documentation for safe passage to the EU. I've contacted an old friend of mine with whom you can stay for a few months; I trust you'll find new accommodations by then," Sebastian said candidly. "I also included the coordinates to a hidden cash reserve in Southern Italy, if the € 50,000 is not enough."

Noa stared at him, eyes wide. "...What?"

"I know you understand what I'm saying, Noa. It's my contingency plan."

"But I thought..." Noa's sentence trailed off. What did he think? What did he expect? Despite his best efforts, he felt a lump materializing in his throat. "I don't want to leave!"

On the verge of exhaustion and unable to stand seeing Noa cry, Sebastian turned to the window again. "I will tell you as I told the others," he said, voice strained with heartache. "I've made my decision."

"Where will *you* go? I can come with you! I'll follow you anywhere," Noa pleaded, taking a step toward him. "Please? I'm so sorry – please don't hate me."

Sebastian closed his eyes, resisting the urge to collapse. "I don't hate you, Noa. But I'm going alone."

The edges of his vision blurring, Noa sank into a sea of hopelessness. He wanted nothing more than to grab Sebastian's hand and prevent him from leaving. Hold on so tightly that the two would never be separated again.

But he knew it would be in vain. Whether he took the envelope or not, flew to Europe or not, he knew that Sebastian would disappear without a trace as soon as he left the building.

"Please," he tried once more. "Don't go. Don't leave me again."

Sebastian shook his head with a weary breath. "Goodbye, Noa."

FIFTEEN
SEPTEMBER

- 10 Months Later. Toronto, Canada -

"Now arriving at: Queen. Queen Station. Doors will open on the right."

Swarms of purses, briefcases, fall coats and umbrellas, limbs and distracted bodies rushed out of and onto an awaiting subway train, packing the cars full.

Seats filled quickly as the automated recording spoke again.

"Please stand clear of the doors. Doors now closing."

The train jerked into motion, picking up speed gradually and welling up with the din of a rush hour crowd. Overlapping conversations, muffled music, coughs and sneezes, shuffling feet and apologies.

"Alex?" A voice sliced through the commuter fog. "Is that you? Oh, my god, it is."

Shaken from his trance, he searched for the source of the sound. "...Miriam?"

"Wow, it's been forever." She approached his corner of

the subway car, pushing past a few passengers and taking hold of the ceiling handle.

"You look great," he blurted out, taking in the sight.

An amused laugh escaped her lips as she re-positioned some shopping bags at her feet. "Wish I could say the same for you, Alex. How much sleep are you getting these days?"

"Not much," he confessed.

Neither of them said anything for a few beats, letting the commuters' chorus fill the silence.

"Now arriving at King. King Station. Doors will open on the right."

"Where are you working now?" Miriam asked. "I heard police."

He nodded in response. "Old buddy of mine put in a good word. Metropolitan HQ. Homicide division."

"Oh, yeah? That's good."

"What about you?" he asked.

"Teaching. Criminology at U of T and the occasional French studies lecture," she said.

Alex raised a brow in surprise. "But you hate young people. You're a professor?"

Miriam jabbed his shoulder teasingly. "Did you want to be a cop?"

"Fair enough," he sighed. "No. Not really."

"It still bothers me to this day, Alex." She leaned forward a bit, lowering her voice. "Why did you do it?"

"Do what? Why did I confess to the oversight committee that I carried out the unwarranted arrest and release of two wanted criminals in a deal with a treasonous underage employee? Or why did I turn over the fortune-telling newspaper to containment?"

Miriam frowned disapprovingly. "Both."

"Now arriving at Union. Union Station. Doors will open on the right."

"It was the right thing to do," he said quietly. "I went into the Intelligence Service mostly because of my oversensitive moral compass. I wouldn't be able to sleep at night otherwise."

"And you can sleep at night now, with a job you can't stand and a life you don't like?" Miriam asked rhetorically.

Alex glanced at her. "Do you hate me?"

"What?" Miriam shook her head, "No, of course not. You suffered the brunt of the punishment from the execs. I quit before they had a chance to terminate me."

"...Seriously?"

"Unbeknownst to you, I took a peek at that Tribune before you gave it away." She reached into her purse and searched for a second, taking out a yellowing slip of paper.

Alex took it from her with a gasp. "No. You didn't."

"I did," she smiled mischievously. "Lady luck loves a good lottery."

"How much?"

She placed a finger over her lips. "Not telling."

Alex chuckled, handing the lotto ticket back. "Of course. So, if they didn't fire you, why did you quit? You could have said you had nothing to do with the cover up. Colson liked you."

"Now arriving at St. Andrew. St. Andrew Station. Doors will open on the right."

"Wasn't the same without you, I guess." Miriam let her gaze drift to the window. "This is my stop."

Alex let go of the handlebar he was holding and cleared his throat. "Are you, uh, free for dinner tonight?"

She smirked, picking up her bags. "Thought you'd never ask."

- Charleston, South Carolina -

"Lottie, please wash those strawberries carefully, 'kay? I got them from the market this morning!" With a chime, the front doors welcomed their proprietress back into her domain. "We can make some fresh smoothies from them."

"Yes ma'am!" A teenage girl with bright yellow pig tails took the basket of berries in her arms, carrying it to the sink.

"And Ollie – please move those chairs out front! They're crowding up the joint."

"Yes ma'am!" A slightly older boy in a baseball cap and an abundance of freckles got to rearranging the furniture.

A sunny November morning rose over the palm trees and boardwalks of Charleston, slowly warming with daylight. Though it hadn't opened yet, a few passing locals and tourists were starting to peek into the display windows of a new establishment near the Ravenel Waterfront park.

Its colorful patio displayed a sign, excitedly announcing The Big Dipper's GRAND OPENING – TODAY! A few select menu items were highlighted on the display, including big and little dipper cones of many flavors, and a limited-time special: The Aurora Polaris ice cream float.

"Elli, there's some folks here to see ya," the boy said, peeking in through the front door. "They say you know 'em?"

Pushing past him, the first visitor rushed inside enthusiastically. "Elli!"

Throwing off her apron, she hopped over the counter. "Mikey! You found it!"

They exchanged hugs, pulling Lucy and Nick in when they entered the shop.

"Place looks great," Nick said.

"Why, thank you!" Elli bowed. "I had help. Meet my

little sister and brother," she waved them over. "Charlotte and Oliver. Aren't they precious?" She put her arms around their shoulders.

"Hey guys," Mike said with a grin. "Nice having your big sis back, right?"

"Kinda," Charlotte replied. "But she's a bit bossy."

"I'll show you bossy," Elli threatened as the teens ran off. She sat on the counter with a fond sigh. "It's so good to see y'all. Thanks for coming to my grand opening."

"Wouldn't miss it," Lucy said with a small smile.

"Oh, did you get a package recently?" Mike asked. "We all got a weird delivery from abroad with no name or return address over the last few weeks."

Elli bent down, reaching under the counter. "Sure did! Arrived about a month ago." She took out a parcel, flipping it on its side. "From Monaco. Haven't opened it yet."

Lucy lifted the end of her scarf – silky sheer and decorated with an intricate design. "From Barcelona."

"I got a real nice set of cigars sent over some place called Antibes," Nick said. "And Mike got some designer shit from Spain, right? Marbella?"

Mike nodded. "You should open yours, El'!"

"Y'all do know who's sending these gifts, right?" Elli carefully tore open the package, retrieving its contents. "Oh, wow!"

Nick whistled. "Sweet poker set. They would know how to make 'em in Monaco."

She placed the golden briefcase on her lap. "I miss him."

"We all do, El'," Mike said, putting his hands in his pockets. "Clearly, he knows where we are! He's tellin' us that we're not alone."

The front door jingled as Oliver peeked in once more.

"Elli, there's a lady sitting on the patio. I told her we weren't open yet but she's not leavin'."

Elli groaned. "S'okay, Ollie. I'll be right back, guys!" She hid her new gift behind the counter and went to the front, stepping out to the patio.

A lone customer was seated on a pale blue chair by the display sign, studying the menu.

"Excuse me," Elli said curtly. "The grand opening isn't 'till—"

Her words caught in her throat.

"Juliette?"

- Gulf of Finland -

The far end of the ferry's cargo hold was cold and damp. Every wave brought with it a slight sway of the container, and the air was textured heavily with dust.

Noa shivered, his exhales producing small puffs of visible smoke with every breath. Seated upon a stranger's suitcase, he hid his hands in his sleeves and repositioned the laptop that was carefully balanced on his knees. A cube with an engraved 11 dangled from its side, connected by a cable.

The MS Princess Anastasia was a grand vessel, operating as both a mini cruise ship and a ferry with impressive guest cabins and deluxe accommodations. Regrettably, the same praise could not be offered for the conditions of her storage bins.

But Noa made this choice impulsively, without the necessary Visa documentation. Sneaking onto the ferry turned out to be much easier than the sleeper train in Copenhagen.

A few hours after the boat departed from the shores of

Stockholm, Noa realized he was not the only illegal stowaway in the Anastasia's cargo. There was another vagrant in the storage container, huddled up with a wool blanket in the opposite corner. The stranger, a woman in a floral shawl, awoke from a restless nap and yawned.

"Ah," she mumbled, noticing Noa and rubbing the sleep from her eyes. *"Govorish' po Russki?"*

Noa glanced up from his screen at the stranger. "Um. *Nyet?*"

The woman sat up against a stack of luggage. "English?"

He nodded.

"Okay. No scare, me no gypsy." She pulled the purse she was using as a pillow onto her lap. "Want *pirozhok?*" Opening the bag, she retrieved a container of rounded baked buns which appeared to be stuffed with filling.

Noa's stomach grumbled at the sight and he nodded again, more eagerly. "Yes, please!"

With a light laugh, the woman moved over as the redhead brought his laptop and took a seat beside her.

"Yana," she said, motioning to herself with the bun before handing one to him. "You?"

"Noa," he replied, hungrily biting into the stuffed pie. Though cold, the savory pastry was delicious, filled with mushrooms and cabbage and enclosed in soft, moist dough.

Yana smiled, watching the boy while eating her own. "Good, *da?*"

"'Fank you," Noa said with a full mouth.

She shifted to sit cross-legged and peered at his computer, open before him on the floor. "What that? Playing game?"

He shook his head, wiping some crumbs from his chin. "No, I wish." He brought the computer back onto his lap, angling the screen for her to see.

"Ah, *karta*," she said. "How you say *karta*? Atlas?"

"Map. I'm looking for someone."

Yana's features wrinkled with worry. "You lost? Lost child?"

"No, no," Noa corrected quickly. He scratched the back of his head, searching for a proper term. "I guess I did lose a person. But I'm not lost. I'm trying to find that person."

"Hm." She studied the map. "Here?" She pointed to a blue dot, flickering on and off in the Baltic Sea.

"I hope so," he said, a twinge of desperation in his voice. "I really hope so."

Yana leaned against the luggage again. "How you know? No wi-fi here."

"I just need satellite now," Noa said. "It's a long story. I didn't even think it would work."

"Much time," she said with a shrug.

Noa watched the blue blinking dot. "Well, um. I've been trying to find this person for months now. But how do you find someone that doesn't want to be found?"

"He is spy?" Yana asked with a gasp.

Noa cringed at the irony. "No. He just... left. And I need to find him."

Yana hummed in understanding.

"Anyway," he continued. "I had a pretty good feeling he would be in Europe, but absolutely no access to his digital presence. So, I made an assumption that he would make a very unique, expensive purchase at some point, and scoped down my search."

"What he buy?" Yana asked, intrigued. "Car? House? Jewels?"

"Boat. I sent out these sticky ID mining packages to the registration software used by every superyacht port in Europe – Monaco, Malta, Montenegro – and set them to notify me at the appearance of a yacht matching my criteria." Noa bit his lip. "It appeared a few months ago. I can't be 100% certain, but the name and subsequent sailing trajectory line up."

Lost at the majority of her stowaway companion's explanation, Yana simply nodded.

"Next, I had to count on his crew's recklessness to download a foreign bridge control upgrade package so I could track their navigation." He tapped on the dot triumphantly. "I've had him since Le Havre. For the past 1,800 nautical miles, through the English Channel and the North Sea until the Baltic."

"Long travel," she said.

"Yeah. But I know where he's going," Noa said with an anxious inhale. "I'm almost certain of it. And I'll beat him to his next port."

- St. Petersburg, Russia -

A hush hung over the port of St. Petersburg. Usually bustling with activity in the warmer months and white nights, and alive with festivities over the winter holidays, a chilled November morning brought with it few tourists or early pedestrians.

Sebastian disembarked from *Aurora IV* and stepped onto the grounds of his hometown. He closed his eyes and looked blindly skyward, listening for the faint melodies of distant memories.

The sounds of car horns. An old radio. A child's cries. He opened his eyes.

The pale, late Autumn sun whispered the snow would soon be coming. Sebastian pulled up the collar of his coat against the harsh harbor wind and made his way into the city.

Though it had been over two decades since he last walked these streets, he was struck by the familiarity of his surroundings. Without drawing attention to himself, Sebastian expertly navigated the city, crossing the Neva river and into the *Kalininsky* district.

Certainly, though some names and signs had changed, the routes were unforgettable. Like it or not, they were etched forever in his mind. In a couple hours, he found himself in a more desolate part of town, walking past dilapidated apartment complexes, boarded up with wooden planks indicating their destruction to make way for new developments.

Turning a corner, distracted by his thoughts, Sebastian felt an unexpected grip on his arm.

A hooded stranger pulled him into an alleyway forcefully, shoving him against a cement wall. *"Koshelek i chasy,"* the assailant demanded in Russian, revealing the glint of a knife inside his coat sleeve.

Surprised at first, Sebastian's reaction morphed into annoyance. "No."

Baffled at the defiance, the hooded man exposed the knife and waved it threateningly. "Wallet and Rolex," he repeated, this time in heavily accented English.

Sebastian withheld a laugh. "Marvelous homecoming," he said under his breath, reaching inside his own coat and drawing a gun. With an extended arm, he pressed it to the mugger's forehead, releasing the safety.

As expected, the man went rigid, dropping the knife in an instant. He backed away slowly, uttering apologies in Russian. When Sebastian didn't pursue, he broke into a run and disappeared into a side street.

Putting the gun away with a disappointed shake of his head, Sebastian continued his journey. Within a few more kilometers, he arrived at his destination.

Standing in the ruins of a crumbled building, he climbed over unstable brick and rubble towards a modest but unmistakable cemetery. He kneeled down beside a short tombstone, carefully wiping dirt and dust off its epitaph with a handkerchief.

Ekaterina Solovyova. 01.15.1988 – 02.02.1992.

Sebastian placed a gloved hand on the tombstone. "Hi Katya," he said, unsure of his own voice. "I'm sorry it took me so long to visit. And I apologize for the English – my Russian isn't what it used to be."

He glanced around the rubble, ensuring solitude. Then, sitting down against the tombstone, he retrieved a small pink box from his coat pocket. "I brought you a gift," he said, unwrapping the box and taking out a pair of petite ballet shoes.

"Remember, for your fourth birthday, you begged and begged for ballerina slippers? Mom secretly passed me some coins the night before, but I didn't have the heart to tell her it was not enough," he said, hanging the shoes over the headstone by their pearly white laces.

"So, I stole them." He watched the slippers sway with the wind. "The pair you loved and wore endlessly for weeks. The pair you're wearing now. What would you have thought of me, I wonder?"

Sebastian put his hands in his pockets. "What must you

think of me now? I couldn't protect you. Couldn't protect those closest to me. My childhood friend, my team, my protégé. It was foolish to believe I could impart any meaningful difference on the world that wasn't negative... I deserve to stand alone."

He stood with a sigh, gently touching the name on the headstone again. "I'm sorry, Katya. But if you'll excuse me, I need to find someplace to get outrageously drunk. I'll come back another day."

Returning to the wreckage of the building, Sebastian climbed back over the ruins. He paused at the remnants of what appeared to be a church bench and sat down, suddenly overcome with fatigue.

Placing his head in his hands, he closed his eyes for just a moment. The moment turned into a few, which turned into minutes, and then, unintentionally, he dozed off.

Evening was falling over the graveyard and its adjacent ruins when Sebastian awoke to a sudden noise.

He sat up straight, readying a hand over his concealed weapon, and listened intently for the footsteps of a supposed intruder. While the church's walls were mostly crumbled, they were high enough to conceal the area directly in front of him.

Sebastian rose slowly, concentrating on the sound of shoes hitting stone. *Not an animal,* he thought with some concern.

"Who's there?" he shouted, taking out the pistol preemptively. An echo of his voice bounced off the walls. He caught a glimpse of something bright red through a crack in the collapsing brick.

Sebastian lowered his gun in disbelief. "...Noa?"

His suspicions were confirmed when a familiar face emerged hesitantly from behind the wall.

"Um, yeah." Noa stood a few feet away, arms wrapped around himself, shivering uncontrollably. "Hi."

Sebastian blinked the sleep out of his eyes. "How did you find me?" He looked around the sparse ruins and empty graveyard with growing realization. "Rather, how long have you been following me?"

"Physically? Since you left the port," Noa sniffed. "Technically, I've been tracking your location since northern France."

"Right. That's troubling," Sebastian admitted. "Why are you here?"

"...You look different."

"Pardon?"

"Your hair," the boy replied.

Sebastian lifted a single strand between gloved fingers. Blond roots peeked out underneath a faded darker shade. "Ah. The color takes a while to come out, but I got tired of the upkeep. Anyway, that's not relevant. Why are you here, Noa?"

He contemplated his answer for a few seconds. "Could you, um, maybe put down the gun first?"

"What? Oh..." Sebastian placed the gun on the ground beside him. "I wasn't—"

In the moment that followed, Noa dropped his backpack and quickly closed the distance between them, trapping the other in a tight hug.

"Wh—hey!" Nearly falling over, Sebastian took a step to regain his balance.

Noa said nothing, hiding his face in Sebastian's coat.

Unsure at the proper response, he put his arms around

the redhead to share some warmth, feeling each tremble emanating from his cold body.

"What are you doing here, Noa?" he asked for a third time.

"Why is it so cold!" Noa whined, teeth chattering. "Russia is even worse than Canada."

Sebastian pushed him back a bit with a frustrated sigh. He removed his coat and draped it over Noa's shoulders. "There. Now stop avoiding my question."

"...Okay. Sorry." Noa pulled the coat over himself closer. "I'm here because I wanted to find you. I've been trying for months. I followed your instructions, but I didn't think your 'old friend' would be Maria! She is so scary, and I got sick of borscht, and I was miserable. I felt so bad about ruining your plans and destroying your team and I know you never want to see me again and that you hate me, but I had to find you and tell you that I—" he took a quick breath, "I don't think I can live without you so please forgive me!"

Taken aback, Sebastian simply said: "Oh."

"I hacked your boat's navigation," Noa added. "I'd been on the lookout for any Aurora's getting registered in Europe. When I saw it was sailing to St. Pete's, I knew it must be you." He gripped the jacket with trembling fingers. "Um. I really am sorry. How can I make you stop hating me?"

"I don't hate you. Not at all." Sebastian put his hand on Noa's head softly. "I cannot fathom why you'd travel so far to find me. I could not hold myself to a single promise. You, on the other hand, can accomplish so much. Your skill is limitless."

Noa shot him a look. "Are you saying I'm *wasting my potential?*"

Sebastian went quiet.

"I spoke to July," Noa said, watching him with a fierce

determination. "She told me everything. About November, the circumstances of his death, and your departure. She also told me that Emilio searched for you years after you left, until he stopped all at once five years ago."

Removing his hand, Sebastian folded his arms across his chest. "Five years... They must've found the note I left you under the floorboard. That would mean he knew my whereabouts since 2009. How does she know this?"

"They stayed in touch after she graduated. Emilio wanted July to 'bring you to justice'."

Sebastian scoffed. "Naturally."

Noa's grasp on the coat tightened. "It gets better. When you and Elli brought July aboard the Deadhorse project, she had an awakening of sorts. Realized the errors of her ways, whatever. I think she's clean now and trying to reconcile with Elli. But here's the kicker: she shared the Deadhorse concept with Emilio at kickoff. Since it turned out you weren't so bad."

"Let me get this straight," Sebastian rubbed his eyes. "Emilio has been keeping tabs on me for years and Juliette kept him informed of my plans...?"

"I graduated last year, yeah? CSIS was my placement. The financial & organized crime unit, to be precise," Noa said. "CSIS already had a case open on the Great Lakes collective when I arrived, but I had made the connection. I was the missing piece needed to find you."

Sebastian sat back down on the bench. "Emilio sicced you on me... despite knowing my intentions."

Noa let him digest the information, watching his expression change.

"And Canadian Intelligence because..." he shook his head incredulously. "Of course. July had defected to my side. She would have found you in any US agency."

"They must've been counting on me to use whatever leads CSIS already had to stop you," Noa said. "Regardless of the ultimate goal you were trying to accomplish."

"Well, it worked." Sebastian let out a humorless laugh. "Flawlessly, too."

Noa picked up his backpack, making his way to the beaten bench and sitting down. "I want to show you something." He removed his computer, opening it to show a report on the screen overlayed with a confidential watermark.

"I'm sure you follow the news," he said. "Or maybe you don't. But after the big reveal, mainstream media reporting about Deadhorse fizzled out. Luckily, Agent Lee is a procrastinating idiot and took days to remove my access, giving me time to plant a backdoor."

"Impressive." Sebastian peered at the screen.

"The impact is there," Noa insisted, switching between a series of graphs and tables. "You guys made a real dent in the movement of drugs and arms across and along the border. And if this is what you did on your own, in under five years, imagine what you could do with my help! I'm no magic newspaper but I'm impressive. Your words – not mine."

Sebastian chuckled. "You are persistent, I'll give you that."

"Do you prefer being on your own?" Noa asked sadly.

"Of course not. I cherish my team. And it tore my heart out, leaving you behind," he replied.

"Then don't!" Noa reached into his bag again.

"What are you doing now?"

"My last-ditch effort, if nothing else worked to convince you." He held out a box of Belgian chocolates. "These were your favorite, right? The ones you kept hidden in our room."

Sebastian took the box wordlessly, touched by the simple gesture.

"When I was in your office once, I found chocolates in the drawer of your desk. You know, when I was, um. Investigating." The redhead lowered his gaze uncomfortably. "I didn't realize at the time why they seemed so familiar."

Standing from the bench, Sebastian took in a deep, defeated breath. "Alright, Noa. No more lies?"

"Never!" Noa leaped to his feet, nearly dropping his bag and computer to the ground.

"No more treachery?"

"No! I promise – swear on my life; on anything!"

"Well then," Sebastian held his hand out, "you win. Consider yourself on a probation period."

Noa shook it wholeheartedly. "You won't regret this!"

"We'll see. But let us take our leave – the cold is getting to me now, too."

Maneuvering out of the ruins, Noa ran ahead with an excited vigor, pulling Sebastian along. They made their way back towards town, through the quieting streets and dimming squares, en route to the port.

"Can I finally go on the yacht?" Noa asked enthusiastically as they approached the harbor.

"I should mention, the Aurora has a strict no smoking policy," Sebastian said with a hint of reprimand. "And no tolerance for clutter."

The teen rolled his eyes. "Whatever, you sound just like Maria. Where are you sailing next?"

"I hadn't decided yet," he replied. "Perhaps it's time we paid old Father Emilio another visit."

"Can we visit Elli, after?"

"Sure. I've been meaning to see her and the others again."

Daylight faded into dusk, casting long, dark shadows over the streets of St. Petersburg. The Neva river, the Winter Palace, the Cruiser Aurora.

The St. Isidore 15th Generation November and 14th Generation September departed from port in the comfortable presence of each other's company and the boundless open sea ahead, carrying in its waves the promise of new adventures.

PART THREE OF THE ST. ISIDORE SERIES

Interested in more St. Isidore adventures? Stay tuned for the next part in this exciting series!

The Hell's Half Acre RETURN

ABOUT THE AUTHOR

This is Daria's first novel, published alongside its prequel, *The Hell's Half Acre Chase*.
Daria lives on the harbor front of Lake Ontario with her husband and elderly Shih Tzu, spending as much time by the water as possible. Born in Russia, she has lived most of her life in Canada.
When she is not writing or listening to Broadway show tunes, Daria works in financial consulting. Both she and her husband also enjoy travelling (outside of global pandemics). Daria's favorite destinations include Mediterranean France & Italy – what a surprise!

Manufactured by Amazon.ca
Acheson, AB